THE COWBOY'S
VALENTINE BRIDE

BY
PATRICIA JOHNS

MILLS &
BOON®

First Published in Great Britain 2017
By Mills & Boon, an imprint of HarperCollins*Publishers*
1 London Bridge Street, London, SE1 9GF

ISBN: 978-0-263-92278-3

23-0217

Our policy is to use papers that are natural, renewable and recyclable products and made from wood grown in sustainable forests. The logging and manufacturing processes conform to the legal environmental regulations of the country of origin.

Printed and bound in Spain
by CPI, Barcelona

Patricia Johns has her honors BA in English literature. She lives in Alberta, Canada, with her husband and son, where she writes full-time. Her first Mills & Boon novel came out in 2013, and you can find her books in the Love Inspired, Western Romance and Heartwarming lines.

To my husband and our little boy—
the two sweetest Valentines in the world.

Chapter One

Brody Mason's leg throbbed. The last of his morphine had worn off, and no matter what position he adopted in front of the crackling fireplace in his childhood home, the pain was constant.

He'd been honorably discharged from the army and given a medal for bravery—presented to him in the crisp hospital bed where he'd spent the last couple of months—but he'd never felt less deserving. While people at home called every returning soldier a hero, he saw a difference: real heroes got their buddies out alive, and Brody hadn't managed to do that. Now he was home in the tiny town of Hope, Montana, and while his family doted on him, no one really under-stood. His fellow soldiers hadn't survived the explo-sion that tore up his leg in early December; he was supposed to have their backs. And that hurt worse than the shrapnel.

The hospital stay had been a haze of pain meds, and every week the doctor assured him he'd be able to leave soon, but then something would hold up his recovery. Brody had missed his sister's wedding because of an infection in his leg, and he'd been forced to watch her nuptials via webcam, which was just as well, considering that he solidly disapproved of her choice in groom. Once he recovered from the leg infection, there was a bronchial infection triggered by all the dust he'd breathed for the last year in Afghanistan, which put off his second surgery to remove the last of the shrapnel. When the surgery was complete, the nurses stopped hovering quite so much—a good sign.

Then one day in late January, a week after his last surgery, the doctor had deemed him sufficiently recovered and signed his discharge papers. Just like that. No muss, no fuss, no grandeur. His parents picked him up from the hospital and drove him home. Which left him here, sitting in front of the fireplace, trying to find a comfortable position for his aching leg.

The back door to the ranch house opened and shut, and there was the soft murmur of voices. He couldn't make out who the nurse was...not that it mattered. He shifted again, closing his eyes against the wave of pain. Brody heard a noise behind him, and he reluctantly turned.

Kaitlyn Harpe stood at the door to the sitting room, her arms crossed over her chest. Her auburn hair hung in loose waves around her shoulders, dark eyes fixed on him uncertainly. She looked nervous to be here—and rightfully so.

"You? Seriously?" Brody wasn't normally this much of a jerk, and he resented the words as soon as they came out of his mouth, but with the pain, his verbal filter seemed to be missing.

"I get that I'm not your first choice, but there aren't a whole lot of nurses available in Hope," she replied with a small smile.

Yeah, that was an understatement. Hope, Montana, was a small ranching community, and while there were two large animal veterinarians in town, medical care for people was a little sparser. Before Kaitlyn went to nursing school, her aunt Bernice was the only other nurse in town. He'd half expected to see the older woman.

Under different circumstances, he might have considered himself lucky. He'd known Kate for years and thought of her as a little sister. She'd always been sweet with a quirky sense of humor, and until recently, he would have described her as honest, too, but she'd gone along with the lie his friends and family had told him while he was away—namely that he still had a fiancée. But Nina had married his best friend, Brian, while he'd been dodging bullets in Afghanistan, and everyone had kept silent about that little fact…so silent that he'd never suspected a thing. No one told him the truth until he'd been in the VA hospital in Fort Harrison for over a month. He'd been set to be released for Dakota and Andy's wedding when that nasty infection set in. Nina still hadn't visited, and he'd had enough. That was when his family admitted that Nina had married Brian a few months back.

And now Nina's sister was going to be his nurse

while he recovered? It was adding insult to injury—literally.

Brody looked past Kaitlyn to where his mother stood in the kitchen, stoically ignoring them. His mother, Millie, wore an apron over a pair of jeans and a long-sleeved turtleneck, and she was rolling out some dough on the island with enough muscle to wrestle down a steer. Whatever she was baking would be leather by the time she was done with it.

"It's good to see you." Kaitlyn came into the room, those big brown eyes fixed on him with a conflicted expression. "I missed you."

"Yeah?"

"Of course. No one else lets me cheat at poker."

She was making a joke, but he wasn't in the mood. She'd been more than a silent bystander to the deception. She'd written him emails every couple of weeks since the day he left, and never once did she let on that anything had changed. At the end of every email, she'd said the same thing: *Nina sends her love.*

"You didn't think to tell me I was writing love letters to a married woman?" he asked. He didn't have strength for pleasantries right now. They might as well get down to it.

How many letters had he obliviously written to Nina since her marriage? Had she laughed at his humble attempts to put his heart on paper while he was out there in the desert? All of this while Nina's own sister hadn't even hinted that he might want to take a closer look.

"Your parents said—" she began.

"You all made a fool of me," he interrupted. "If I'd known she was starting up with Brian, I could have saved myself some humiliation."

"And if after you learned the truth you lost heart out there and you'd been shot?" she demanded, something close to anger sparkling in those eyes. "We'd have blamed ourselves."

"You could have blamed Brian and Nina." He shot her a sardonic smile. "I do."

Kaitlyn's eyes misted and she shot him an irritated look. "You aren't funny, and if you'd been dead, the moral high ground wouldn't have been much comfort. No one wanted to keep the secret, you know. We all felt terrible about it—"

"Except Nina, of course." He couldn't help the bitterness in his tone. Nina had been busy getting married to another guy…and not just any guy—his best friend.

"Brody, I'm not my sister." Something in her voice gave him pause, and he heaved a sigh. No, she wasn't her sister, and Nina was the one who started this whole thing, but Kaitlyn could have gone against the tide and leveled with him.

"It's just that, of all people, Kaitlyn, I figured I could count on you to tell me the truth. There were a few times when I got suspicious, but then I'd get an email from you, and I'd think that it was okay because I could trust you. You'd fill me in if there was something I needed to know. But Nina always sent her love, right?"

Kaitlyn blushed and looked away for a moment.

They'd been friends. He'd called her his "overly serious Kate" because she'd taken her studies so seriously, and he'd always tried to distract her while he waited for Nina to get ready to go out. He'd always won that tussle between responsibility and fun, and she'd push her books aside and turn those chocolate brown eyes on to him. Having her full, overly serious attention had felt good—too good. But he knew the line and he'd never flirted with it. Nina had always taken forever to get ready, but Kaitlyn made the wait fun. They'd laughed at the same jokes and talked about life, and he'd given her advice on some boyfriend who wasn't up to snuff. And of all people, he'd trusted Kaitlyn to be above that kind of deception.

"We all protected *you*," Kaitlyn said after a moment. "It wasn't ideal, I get that, but it was all we could think of. Whether you believe it or not, we were doing this because we wanted you home safe." She crouched in front of the foot stool where his leg rested. "Speaking of which, let me take a look."

Brody sighed and nodded his approval. It wasn't like he had much choice anyway. He obviously needed a nurse to aid his recovery, and as she'd pointed out, he couldn't exactly be picky.

Her touch was light and discreet as she uncovered the bandaged wounds. He'd been lucky—no broken bones—but the shrapnel had gone deep into the muscle and the multiple surgeries to retrieve it had left the doctors uncertain if there would be nerve damage or not. That thought scared him. He was born on a ranch and raised on horseback. What was he going to do if he had nerve damage? Riding a horse or returning to the army, he'd need this leg to cooperate. Maybe the fact that it hurt so badly was a good sign—nerves screaming their existence, if nothing else.

"I still can't believe Dakota married Andy," Brody said bitterly, wincing as the gauze caught on some stiches. When he'd left, his sister thoroughly loathed Andy, and now they were married. Everything had changed in one short year, and home felt foreign.

Kaitlyn replaced the gauze and taped it back down. "Something happened on that cattle drive—that's all we know. What can you do?"

"He single-handedly ruined our land," Brody said. "She can't be in love with him."

Kaitlyn rocked back on her heels and eyed Brody for a long moment until he looked away. Then she sighed and pushed herself to her feet.

"A lot has changed," she said quietly. "And I don't even know if you're glad to be back or not, but I'm glad."

"Are you?" She looked like the same old Kaitlyn— gentle, sweet, doe-eyed—and yet she was different, too. She was stronger, more confident somehow. Situations had changed, but so had people.

"I am." She fixed him with her direct stare. "So you go ahead and be mad at this whole blasted town because I'm happy you're back in once piece."

"Give or take," he said with a wry smile.

Kaitlyn smiled and shook her head. "I'm going to get your prescription for pain meds refilled, and over the next few days we're going to get you walking."

She looked down at his medication log. "You're due for another dose in an hour."

"The sooner the better on those meds, Kate. It hurts pretty bad."

"Okay." She looked as if she wanted to say something more, then gave him a nod and turned back toward the kitchen.

Brody gritted his teeth and gently lowered his leg to the floor. The pain was so intense that it turned his stomach, but he wasn't about to lie around bemoaning his tattered state. He needed to recover, because once he was back in shape again, he knew exactly where he was going.

This ranch and this town didn't hold anything for him anymore. He was going back to the army to finish what he started. In the army the truth had been ugly, but no one had lied to him.

WHEN KAITLYN RETURNED from the drug store with Brody's pain prescription, Dakota opened the door for her. Kaitlyn stepped into the warm kitchen, fragrant with baking bread. The last time she'd been in this room, they'd been having a meeting of sorts—the Mason family and the Harpes. That was the evening when Mr. Mason outlined the plan to get Brody home safe. Nina and Brian had already moved to the city, so Kaitlyn's father, Ron, filled Nina in on her part of the deal later—to keep her relationship with Brian a secret and to answer Brody's emails so he wouldn't suspect anything. It had been an order, not a request. Nina hadn't wanted to go along with it—she was about to get married, after all, and she wanted to announce it to the world. But if she announced it, then Brody would hear all about it, and that could be devastating. Brody had to be the priority, and Nina would just have to get married quietly.

Kaitlyn hadn't been back to this ranch since that solemn meeting of minds, but she and Dakota had run into each other around town a few times, and a tenuous partnership was born. They both wanted Brody home safe—which he was. Kaitlyn could only hope that the deception had been worth it.

"Hi," Kaitlyn said with a quick smile. "I've got the pills."

"How's his leg?" Dakota asked. "He wouldn't let me see it. Said he'd wait for a medical professional because I didn't know squat."

Kaitlyn smiled wanly—that sounded like Brody, always the tough guy. Maybe he'd been trying to protect his sister—that leg wasn't pretty.

"It's...not great." His leg, from thigh to calf, was covered in jagged cuts and stitches. Some of the wounds had already healed over—more or less—from his first surgeries, but others were fresh from retrieving the deeper, harder-to-reach shrapnel. She could tell how much pain Brody was in, and if his leg got infected again, it could be fatal. He'd been right about one thing—proper medical care was a necessity if he wanted to walk again.

"He's mad," Dakota said. "About Nina and all that."

Kaitlyn was still angry with her sister about her in-

fidelity. Brody was strong, sweet, handsome, kind...
He was the perfect guy, and Kaitlyn had been in love
with him from afar for a couple of years before he
asked out her sister. But he was two years older than
Kaitlyn, and she hadn't even registered on his radar.
He'd made his choice—a perfectly understandable
one. Nina was the beautiful sister—a redhead with
soft green eyes and a voluptuous pinup-girl figure.
She turned heads everywhere she went, and Kaitlyn
hadn't, at least not when her sister was anywhere
near. Kaitlyn was confident in her own looks—she
was beautiful, even—but she'd been quite solidly in
her older sister's shadow.

So why couldn't Nina wait for him? Kaitlyn had
been through it a thousand times. If it had been her,
she'd have waited as long as she had to...but Brody
wasn't hers. He'd never seen her that way, and there
were lines that Kaitlyn would never cross.

"So who had to tell him about Nina?" Kaitlyn
asked. It was the conversation they'd all been dread-
ing.

"Me." Dakota winced. "Just before the wedding.
He kept asking where Nina was, and I think he suspected. I mean, how many fiancées do you know who
don't bother visiting their wounded man in the hospital? When I told him, he just sort of deflated. He
didn't look surprised, just...silent."

"Imagine if that had happened over there," Kaitlyn
reminded her. "Nina's such a selfish—"

"It's done, it's done..." Dakota shook her head.
"And Nina isn't your fault. We're all just trying to pick

up the pieces, and this was the plan, right? He needed to find out here, so we could get him through it."

"He's mad that we hid it." Kaitlyn lowered her voice further.

"I know." They exchanged a long look, then Dakota nodded in the direction of the sitting room. "He's waiting."

Kaitlyn got a glass of water from the sink and headed into the sitting room. Brody was sitting forward, leaning toward the fire. He didn't hear her at first, and he was so close to the flames that they reflected against his face.

Brody had changed since he left—there were lines around his mouth that weren't there before, and his eyes had lost that boyish twinkle. There was nothing boyish left in him—he'd hardened, stilled. If Nina could see what she'd caused… But this wasn't all because of Nina. This was also because of the war. Soldiers saw things that civilians couldn't even imagine, and when they got home again, it sure didn't help to return to a nasty surprise.

Should I have told him?

How could she ever be sure? What she knew was that Brody was home, and her job had just begun.

"Here are your pills," Kaitlyn said, setting the glass of water next to him and unscrewing the cap to the bottle. "Now, it's important that you never take more than the recommended dose of these. They're strong."

"I'm not suicidal." Brody held out his hand for

the pills, then tossed them back with a sip of water. "Thanks."

"I was more concerned with addiction," she retorted.

Brody laughed softly. "I'm not an addict, either."

"Good."

He turned toward her, dark eyes locking on to her face. "Did you think I'd change that much?"

Brody had been a fun-loving guy with an infectious laugh. He'd been tall and muscular, but he'd bulked up even more since he left, and his lean muscle had turned hard and thick. His hair had been a tousled mess of glossy curls, and now he had that standard-issue army buzz cut—but it didn't hurt his looks any. It seemed to suit the new him.

"I don't know," she replied honestly. "Life changes everyone, and you've seen more than most."

"Yeah, well…" He leaned back in his chair, wincing as he got settled. "You've changed, too."

"Have I?" She grabbed his medications chart and wrote in his dose. "I feel like the only one who hasn't changed around here."

"You grew up." His voice was low and quiet. "When I left, you were a kid."

"When you left, I was a woman," she replied evenly. She'd been twenty-two when he left for the army, and that hardly constituted a "kid." But she'd never looked quite as womanly as Nina had. Nina had eclipsed her quite easily, it seemed, all pouty lips and swaying hips. Kaitlyn hadn't had a chance. She had been a tamer version of her sister in every way.

Her hair was dark auburn compared to Nina's fiery red, and her figure was slim, her breasts smaller, her expression direct and frank. Nina had a way of looking up through her lashes that stopped men in their tracks. When Kaitlyn was a teenager, she'd tried to imitate her older sister's sultry pout in the mirror, and she'd cracked herself up. She looked ridiculous, and she'd decided then and there to simply be herself— a brave stance for someone in the shadow of Hope, Montana's sexiest available woman.

But not so available anymore.

While Kaitlyn had resented what her sister did to Brody, having Nina both married and moved to the city had been a strange relief. For the first time in her life, Kaitlyn felt like she could breathe a little deeper, expand a little more. With Nina in the room, there had hardly seemed to be enough oxygen for the both of them—and what Nina wanted, Nina got.

"Last year I missed our dads' birthdays," Brody said after a moment. "I kept thinking of the feast you all would be eating."

Kaitlyn's father, Ron, and Brody's father, Ken, had birthdays in the same week. The men had been close since elementary school. For as long as Kaitlyn could remember, both families had been celebrating those February birthdays together with a trail ride and a massive meal.

"Last year half of us got food poisoning, so you weren't missing out on as much as you thought," she replied with a wry smile. "Someone thought clams would be a great birthday meal. Wow. It was bad...

The trail ride didn't happen. Brian landed in the hospital with some Gravol on IV."

"You emailed me about that." His smiled slipped, and she knew what he was thinking. She shouldn't have mentioned Brian. She grimaced.

"Nothing had happened then between Brian and Nina—that I knew of, at least," Kaitlyn said. "We were all friends with Brian, you know that."

"Yeah. Solid guy." Brody's tone dripped sarcasm, and Kaitlyn couldn't blame him.

They remained silent for a couple of minutes, and Kaitlyn remembered how different everything had been a year ago. They'd been proud of Brody, and scared for him. They'd been happy about Nina and Brody's engagement. Nina had spent hours staring at the ring on her finger, and Kaitlyn had been determined to sort through her own feelings of jealousy privately. She was happy for her sister—of course, she was—and she'd never really believed that Brody would look twice at her with Nina in the same hemisphere anyway. But it still stung, knowing she was destined to be half in love with her brother-in-law for the foreseeable future.

"Are you all still doing the trail ride this year?" Brody asked.

"I imagine so," Kaitlyn replied. "It's tradition, isn't it?"

"Good," he said. "I'm going to ride, too."

Kaitlyn frowned, silently considering the options. Trail rides were narrow and bumpy, and she couldn't responsibly give him enough pain meds to dull that kind of agony. He seemed to read her thoughts.

"It isn't hard riding by any stretch. You know that, Kate. I've been riding since before I could walk, and I'm not sitting back at the house with the cooks."

"You've earned a rest," she said. "You're the resident hero, after all."

"Don't use that word with me." His voice turned gruff and stony. "I'm riding. Period."

There was no invitation for discussion. He'd been through a nightmare in Afghanistan, and she could only guess at the memories he carried with him. He wanted to heal and recover, and that solidity of mind was important. They'd just have to work toward his goal. Even if he wasn't strong enough to ride in time, he'd at least have something to work toward. And once it got closer to the trail ride, he'd be able to see the futility of putting his body through that kind of punishment. There was no use in breaking his spirit now.

"You want to ride?" she said with a smile. "All right. That's our goal. Let's see what we can do."

"Good." Brody smiled faintly. "And I'm serious, Kate. Don't go easy on me."

"I had no intention of it," she retorted. "I'll be a regular drill sergeant. You'll think longingly of your boot camp days."

Brody chuckled, then sighed. "Why am I so tired all of a sudden?"

"It's the pills. Sleep is good for you. Get some rest."

Brody nodded and leaned his head against the back of the chair. She quelled the urge to brush a hand against his forehead. She didn't want to go hard on Brody—she wanted to give him the safe, warm place to heal that he so desperately needed, but he didn't want those things from her. That had been Nina's domain.

Kaitlyn would have to get over these feelings for him, because a future with Brody was an absolute impossibility. Before it was because he was engaged to her sister, and now, even with Nina safely out of the picture, anything developing between them was equally impossible.

Kaitlyn had lived in her sister's shadow her entire life, and she refused to stay there in the heart of the man she loved.

On the fireplace mantle, a tattered slip of red paper caught her eye. She paused, stepped closer to look and a lump rose in her throat as she recognized it—a kid's vintage Valentine's card that she'd slipped into his luggage before he left for boot camp. They used to joke about the little sayings on those cards— corny lines that could end up being eerily prophetic. So she'd slipped one in his bag that said, "You're brave, Valentine." It went along with a joke they'd shared that it took a big man to take on a woman as high maintenance as Nina was. She thought he'd get a laugh out of it...but it looked like he'd done one more than that, and had kept it.

Kaitlyn shut her eyes against the wave of emotion. How she'd longed to say more than "You're brave." She'd wanted to say, "You hold my heart." She'd wanted to say, "Do whatever you have to in order to get back here alive."

For now, she'd do her duty and get Brody back in the saddle, or as close to it as she could. And maybe in the process, she'd be able to work through a few of these feelings and put them to rest for good. She had some healing to do, too.

Chapter Two

Brody woke with a start, his heart thudding hollowly in his ears. The dream was still fresh in his mind—fire, explosions, fear mingling with his training. In his dream, he pulled himself across the dusty ground, a trail of fresh blood behind him, and he grabbed at Jeff's hand, only to realize his hand was all that was left of him. He always woke at the same place, with the hand clutched in his, rubbery and limp.

Brody swallowed the bile that rose in his throat, and he sucked in a wavering lungful of air. This had been his first night back home, and he'd slept in the visitor's bedroom on the main floor. There had been no way he was hopping up those stairs last night, and so they'd settled him down here. It was just as well—he wasn't sure how he'd feel about sleeping in his old bedroom anyway. His sister's room was directly above him, and glancing at the clock, he realized that she'd already be out doing chores. It was past four in the morning.

I should be out there, too.

He rubbed his hands over his face and grimaced as

he sat up. His leg throbbed. If things were different, he'd already be out in the frigid January air. He'd be driving out to the herds with a pickup bed full of hay, and he'd bring a shovel to break the ice that would cover the cattle's water troughs. He'd always wanted to join the army, but that hadn't emptied the cowboy out of him. There was something about the crisp air at dawn and the lowing of cattle that soothed his soul like nothing else, and right now, he could use a little soothing, but he hardly felt like he deserved it.

Jeff had had a wife and three small kids waiting for him, and he'd returned home in a box. Jeff's wife would have been given a flag in her husband's honor, and those little kids would never see their dad again. Jeff always had pictures in his pocket, and he'd show them to anyone who would look. Three blond, blue-eyed kids, the youngest of which looked like she could barely walk. So when Brody got back to American soil to find out his fiancée hadn't waited for him, it hardly seemed fair that he should be the one to come back alive.

He just hadn't counted on the dreams. Other guys had mentioned them—the haunting nightmares that came back every time they shut their eyes, but somehow he'd thought he'd be immune. He was tough—but not that tough, apparently.

He grabbed the bottle of pills on his nightstand and shook two into his palm. They'd help with the pain. He'd have to remember what time he took them so he could tell Kaitlyn when she arrived.

Kaitlyn as his nurse was hard to wrap his head

around. She'd been attending nursing school when he left, but he'd never really imagined her in the role. Her aunt, Bernice Harpe, was the local nurse—a solid woman of sixty. Kaitlyn had always been Nina's younger sister to him, sitting with textbooks and paper spread in front of her at the kitchen table. When he thought of Kaitlyn, he saw her with a backpack and her hair pulled into a ponytail. And a year later, she was his nurse—cleaning his wounds, checking his stitches, noting his medication. And she was bossy, too.

Swallowing the pills, he dropped back onto his pillow. Everything had changed since his return. The shock of Nina's marriage was starting to wear off, and while he'd been sure that underneath that shock was some heartbreak and pain, right now he felt relief. He'd been absolutely positive that Nina was the woman for him before he left for the army, but after boot camp and eleven months in the desert with spiders as big as his hand, he'd done a lot of changing, too. He wasn't the same guy who left town a little over a year ago, and while he'd hoped he could pick up where he left off at home, he'd been wrong.

Maybe Nina marrying someone else was for the best. He couldn't really imagine her nursing him back to health anyway. He'd been the one to take care of her, not the other way around. She'd been flirtatious and fun, and incredibly high maintenance. That engagement ring had set him back significantly more than three months' salary. If she'd waited for him, he'd have had to face that look of disappointment when she realized the husband she'd be saddled with—wounded, bitter, broken. Maybe it was all for the best… The pain had dulled—still there but somehow far away—and his eyes drooped shut.

Several hours later, Brody awoke again, this time to a soft tap on his door. He pulled his blanket over his waist to keep himself decent and called, "Yeah?"

The door opened to reveal Kaitlyn. She wore a pair of jeans and a white cotton shirt that brought out the contrast between her milky skin and the auburn waves that fell behind her shoulders. That sure beat waking up to Afghanistan.

"Morning," she said. "How did you sleep?"

"Like the medicated."

"I guess that's to be expected," she said with a chuckle. "What time did you take your pills last night?"

"Four in the morning."

She jotted it down on a chart, then pulled out a roll of gauze. "I'm going to change your dressing this morning. Are you okay with that?"

Her tone was professional and slightly distanced. He might as well be in the hospital again with the kind but unrecognizable nursing staff that moved through his room like clockwork. He didn't like this side to Kaitlyn—and while he appreciated her attempt to put him at ease, maybe he didn't need to be at ease. A few messy, personal connections were better than sterile professionalism, where the emptiness was filled by the clamor of his memories.

"How come you're being so formal?" he asked with a grimace.

"I'm your nurse. You're my patient. It's a different relationship, and you need to be able to trust me for your medical concerns."

"I'd trust you a whole lot more if you didn't sound like a stranger," he said.

Kaitlyn smiled and shrugged—suddenly she looked like the same old Kate who used to beat him at cards.

"That's more like it," he said. "I'm still me, and you're still you."

"Except you have to do as I say," she said, a teasing smile tugging at one side of her lips.

"Yeah, yeah." She was right—he was at a distinct disadvantage...especially waking up to Kaitlyn coming into his room first thing in the morning before he was dressed and steeled to the day. At least it was cold enough that he'd worn an army-issue undershirt to bed so she wasn't staring at him bare chested.

"All right," she said, kneeling next to the bed. "Let's see the leg."

Brody tossed the covers back to expose his leg, and she went to work. She moved with confidence, peeling back bandages, easing gauze away from the wounds. She made little sympathetic sounds when gauze stuck to stitches.

"Wiggle your toes," she instructed.

He complied, and she looked satisfied. "Does that hurt to move them?"

"No."

"Good sign." She took his foot in her hand and moved his ankle in a full rotation, then jotted something in a notebook. "How is the pain right now on a scale of one to ten?"

"Ten being?" he asked, raising an eyebrow.

"When I saw you yesterday," she said.

So she'd noticed how bad his pain was the day before. That was somehow gratifying. He wasn't the complaining type, but he also didn't want to suffer for days unnecessarily, either.

"About a six," he said.

"And you're—" she looked at her watch "—just about due for your next dose. So that's an improvement."

"Why not just ask if I'm feeling any better?" Brody asked.

"Because you'd tell me you were even if you weren't," she retorted.

She had a point. "Okay, fine."

"So now I want you to stand up," she said, pushing herself to her feet. She stood beside the bed, hands folded in front of her and a no-nonsense look on her face.

"What?" He pushed himself up onto his elbows. "Right now?"

"Yes, right now."

"You're not going to give me pain meds first?"

"No." She met his gaze evenly, and Brody heaved a sigh. "If you don't start putting some weight on that leg, it'll only get harder."

Brody pushed the covers back and Kaitlyn bent to help lift his injured limb over the side of the bed. Every movement was a fresh blaze of pain, and he closed his eyes against it, willing his stomach to settle. He felt vulnerable sitting here in an undershirt and a pair of army-issue shorts. His muscles were tense along his shoulders, and he sucked in a sharp breath.

"Take a moment to breathe..." Her voice was quiet and close. "You'll be fine. I'm right here. When you're ready, you'll stand, but you'll put all your weight on your good leg. I'm not that mean."

The pain slowly subsided, and he had to admit it was marginally better than yesterday. She'd said it was a good sign, hadn't she?

"Okay," he said.

Kaitlyn's cool fingers slipped under his biceps and she tugged him gently forward. He followed her encouragement and pushed himself up, all of his weight on his good leg. He wavered slightly, and Kaitlyn moved in closer—sliding an arm around his waist to steady him.

The auburn top of her head shone just at his shoulder level, and he was distinctly aware of where her hands touched his sides, even if he was trying to ignore it. She smelled good—something like vanilla, but not quite—and it made him start thinking of things he should know better than to connect to Kaitlyn Harpe.

"Can you straighten your leg?" she asked, and her voice was close to his chest as she looked down at his injured leg—that was her focus, at least. He straightened it with a grimace, and after a moment, he put a little bit of weight onto it.

That was too much, and the pain made the room

tilt and spin. She'd never be able to catch him if he went down...

"Brody, this is great!" Her tone lost the nurse quality, and she looked up at him with shining eyes. It brought him back to the one time he'd kissed her when he was all of twelve... They'd been kids, and nothing had ever come of it, of course. If he were a little less woozy, he'd be tempted by those pink lips so close to his face—just a matter of dipping his head down and catching them with his—but with the room tilting like that, he'd probably miss. He wouldn't come off as anything better than an awkward twelve-year-old, pecking a girl on the lips and not knowing what else to do.

"I'd better..." His voice was weaker than he liked, but she expertly eased him back down to the side of the bed, and he rubbed his hands over his face. She was his nurse, but having her this close to him was going to be harder than he'd imagined.

"A little dizzy?" she asked.

"A bit."

"That's natural. It'll be easier the next time we do it. You've been on some pretty strong pain medications." She was back to being the nurse again, and she chattered on about his different doses of meds as she adjusted his pillows so that he could sit propped up in bed.

"I think I need a few minutes to myself," he said discreetly.

"Sure." She shot him a grin. "I'll go get your

breakfast sorted out. You shouldn't take any more pills on an empty stomach. Just trust me on that."

She made a grossed out-face; he laughed softly. This was definitely going to be strange to get used to... The Kaitlyn who joked around and made faces was also the woman who was taking care of him. This was going to be a delicate balance, he could tell.

"I believe you," he said.

"I'll be back in a bit." She left the room and closed the door behind her with a click, and he was left in silence.

That quiet felt good. Last night, he'd had all sorts of attention from his family. Everyone had questions, and his mother had wanted to make him comfortable, but only ended up leaving his pillow lumpy behind his back. But he couldn't tell her, because every time she fussed over him, he could see the tears misting her eyes. No matter what had happened over there, she was still his mom, and that was something that hadn't changed. Except that she'd been part of the deception, too, and that rankled him. When he was off serving the country, he should have been able to trust his family to have his back.

But they thought they had.

And maybe that was the biggest problem.

Of all the changes around here—Nina's betrayal, Dakota's marriage, Kaitlyn—he was the biggest change of all, and he wasn't sure he could fit back into his spot here again, even for the short term.

You're brave, Valentine. He'd kept it—a standing joke between them—but it had turned into a kind of good luck charm. He'd tucked that slip of paper into his front pocket because it made him feel braver somehow. A lot of the guys had good luck talismans ...a small stone from their home driveway, or a hair elastic from a girlfriend. He'd had the Valentine card.

In the army, he'd learned that when you were wounded, you had to keep focused on the next step. That might be pulling yourself across the rocky ground, or tying off your own tourniquet. That was what he had to do now with his recovery—grit his teeth and take the next step. The rest of the answers would have to wait.

WHEN KAITLYN HAD arrived at the Mason ranch that morning, Millie Mason was making breakfast—oatmeal with raisins, stacks of toast with butter and boiled eggs. The Mason kitchen always smelled of baking and food, something Nina had resented.

"I'm not a cook," Nina had insisted when Brody said that all he wanted for his birthday was a cake made by his girl. "Why can't he just get his mother to make the cake and let me provide...other things?"

Nina always managed to sound like Marilyn Monroe with her innuendos, but she had had a point. Since when did a fiancée need to replace a mother? But Kaitlyn had sensed that Nina's frustration went deeper than a different skillset—Nina hadn't ever been terribly nurturing. She'd been beautiful, and everyone else had nurtured *her*. Including her sister. Kaitlyn hadn't been so different from everyone else, constantly making excuses for Nina. *Nina isn't*

very good at that. Her heart is in the right place.
But maybe her heart hadn't been quite so well situated after all.

Nina had suggested that Kaitlyn just bake the cake and let Nina take the credit, but Kaitlyn had said no. It was one thing to have her sister dating the guy who had her heart in a vice, and quite another to bake the cake that would make Brody love Nina even more. So Kaitlyn flat out refused...but consented to pick one up at the bakery since Nina wasn't dressed yet. Looking back, Kaitlyn couldn't believe she'd been such a pushover.

Now, as Kaitlyn left Brody in his bedroom and returned to the Mason kitchen, she found it empty, the food on the table and the air fragrant with freshly brewed coffee. This was a kitchen where love took the form of food, and while that was hard for a girlfriend to compete with, it certainly did make for a cozy home. Growing up with Millie Mason's cinnamon buns and strawberry pies would have been idyllic.

"Mrs. Mason?" Kaitlyn called.

There was no answer, so Kaitlyn opened a cupboard and pulled out some bowls and plates to set the table. She wasn't Brody's girlfriend, and she didn't need to prove anything. Her goal was to get Brody to walk from the bedroom to the kitchen, and the best way she could see to make that happen was to lure Brody out with food—and his mother's fantastic cooking was sitting right here waiting.

An envelope crinkled in Kaitlyn's back pocket, and she paused. Nina had sent a letter for Brody just as soon as she found out that he was on his way back. That was the deal—she needed to explain her actions herself, except Kaitlyn had hoped she could do it in person, or at least garner up the courage for a phone call. Regardless, once Brody read it, Kaitlyn was supposed to give her sister a call and let her know. That would let Nina off the hook, and she could start announcing her wedded bliss from the rooftops. Mrs. Brian Dickerson.

Kaitlyn had to admit she was curious about the contents of that letter, but there probably wasn't anything in there that Kaitlyn didn't already know. Nina and Brian had been flirting for some time before Brody even left, not that anyone thought anything of it. Brian had driven Nina home from the airport after they'd all seen Brody off. In fact, Brian had been around a lot, so maybe it shouldn't have been quite so shocking that something had developed between the two of them.

The outside door opened with a rush of cold air.

"Morning," Dakota said as she came inside. She blew out a breath and slammed the door shut again. She pulled off her gloves and unzipped her coat.

"Where are your parents?" Kaitlyn asked.

"They went to my uncle's place. He's come down with a nasty flu, so they're helping out with his chores this morning."

Kaitlyn nodded. Ranches didn't stop for pesky little things like vomiting or fevers. Dakota lifted the lid of the porridge pot and inhaled the aroma. What had Mrs. Mason added—nutmeg? It smelled amazing.

"How's Brody?" Dakota asked.

"I got him standing this morning," she replied.

"Really?" Dakota grinned. "That's great! How long do you think it'll take him to be fully recovered?"

"I'm not sure." Kaitlyn frowned. "That depends on him."

"Hmm." Dakota pulled her hands through her hair. "I know we've probably manipulated things quite enough, but—"

"No," Kaitlyn said firmly. "Leave me out of anything else."

"The thing is, we're going to need Brody around here," Dakota said, ignoring Kaitlyn's statement. "Dad will, at least. With Andy and me living on the Granger ranch, and with Mackenzie busy with the new babies, I can't be running between two ranches forever. I'm exhausted."

Kaitlyn could sympathize. Dakota was a new wife, and she was trying to support the running of two different ranches. It wasn't a fair workload. But then, Brody wasn't exactly a candidate for ranch work, either.

"He's not in any condition to do chores," Kaitlyn said. "Right now, Brody has to focus on recovery."

"It isn't that. The problem is, when I talked to Brody last night, he didn't seem like he wanted to stay," Dakota said. "At all."

Kaitlyn's stomach tightened. Brody wasn't intending to stay in Hope? For some reason, she'd assumed that he was home safe...for good. Obviously, it was a presumptuous conclusion, but she hadn't seriously considered him leaving again.

"I didn't realize," Kaitlyn said quietly.

"So we need to convince him to stay," Dakota said.

"We?" Kaitlyn raised an eyebrow. "Seriously, I'm done with interfering. I highly doubt Brody would welcome our meddling, either."

"He's always liked you—"

"I don't think he likes me as much as you think." She smiled wanly. And he may like her even less after he saw the letter from Nina. She pulled the envelope from her back pocket and tapped it against her hand. "My sister sent a letter to explain things to Brody."

"What did she say?" Dakota asked, lowering her voice.

Kaitlyn shrugged. "No idea. But I have to give it to him. He deserves to hear from her."

Dakota nodded, but she eyed the letter in distrust. "I just wish I knew what she said..."

"We aren't opening it," Kaitlyn said.

"No, of course not." But Dakota looked a tiny bit sheepish. "You have to give it to him."

"The sooner the better, right?" Kaitlyn asked. "I don't want to make things harder on him, but it might actually help him make sense of what happened."

There was a rustle behind them.

"Give me what?"

Both women turned to see Brody in the doorway. He'd managed to get his crutches, but he had to hunch over them. They looked like matchsticks compared to his bulky frame. His expression was taut, and his lips were pale. He was in pain, but he'd managed to get out here on his own, and Kaitlyn couldn't help the grin that came to her lips. She hurried to his side and reached to steady him.

"I'm fine," he grunted. "Let me do it."

Kaitlyn stepped back, feeling slightly stung, not that she entirely blamed him. Dakota pulled out the closest kitchen chair, and Brody sank into the chair with a wince.

"You okay?" Dakota asked her brother. "You look…white."

Brody nodded slowly. He'd be nauseated after that exertion, Kaitlyn knew, and she slid a glass of water in front of him. He took a sip and some of the color came back to his face.

"So what are you supposed to give me, but don't want to part with?" Brody asked, glancing between them.

Kaitlyn sighed and held out the envelope. "A letter from Nina."

Brody eyed the envelope in Kaitlyn's hand, then took it from her, his rough fingers brushing against hers. He looked ready to tear it open, then he sighed and tucked it into his front pocket.

"Aren't you going to read it?" Dakota asked.

"Probably." Brody cast his sister an annoyed look. "What's it to you?"

"I'd kind of like to see what she has to say for herself," Dakota retorted, and when Brody glanced in Kaitlyn's direction, Dakota went on, "Oh, don't worry about Kaitlyn's feelings. We're all pretty much on the same page when it comes to Nina and Brian."

Kaitlyn shrugged—Dakota was right. They'd all hashed through this so many times that the eggshells were no longer necessary. They all thought Nina was a nitwit for what she'd done, and they all knew that there wasn't a thing they could do about it. Nina had made her choice, and they'd all have to live with it. Including Brody.

"Nina wanted to explain, I think," Kaitlyn said, except that Kaitlyn highly doubted Nina's explanation would have the same impact without her big green eyes and plunging cleavage. Nina had always managed to sweet-talk her way out of every scrape, but this one came down to character and cleavage simply didn't make up for that kind of deficiency.

"Fine." Brody's voice was gruff and he reached for the pot. Kaitlyn dished him up some porridge and watched as Brody poured a splash of milk over it.

For all of their plotting and planning, trying to save Brody from the brunt of this, Kaitlyn was now faced with the fresh heartbreak her sister had caused. She could only imagine what Brody was feeling— humiliation, loneliness, disappointment—and she couldn't make it any better. She couldn't bake her sister's cake, and she couldn't replace her sister's love.

She opened the medication bottle and shook out two pills.

Brody accepted them with a nod, and in the split second when his eyes met hers, she saw the depth of his pain. This was the problem with being half in love with her patient—that look in his eyes cut her to the core. If there was any other possibility—if Bernice weren't already working with three elderly patients—Kaitlyn would step back, take some space of her own. But there weren't any other nurses available, and Kaitlyn owed him.

Chapter Three

Brody glanced in the direction Kaitlyn had gone, and he adjusted himself to angle his hip toward the warmth of the crackling fire. The back door opened and shut as Kaitlyn left, and Brody felt the emptiness of the house settle around him. He didn't need constant babysitting, but he was still disappointed to see her go.

I've got to stop that.

He didn't need another woman to take Nina's place, least of all Nina's sister. But that wasn't why he missed Kate. He missed her for all the reasons he'd missed her while he was overseas. She had been a good friend for years, and right now he needed that friendship more than ever.

The fire was comfortingly hot, while outside the window frost crept up the glass like creaking fingers. It was bright and sunny outside, with that pale, watercolor sky that promised extreme cold. This was the kind of day that made a man want to be by a fire anyway.

"I wanted to talk to you," Dakota said, slipping

into the chair opposite him and tucking her feet up under her.

Brody startled and his heart pounded in his throat. "Don't do that to me."

"Do what?" Dakota asked.

"I didn't know you came in." Things that didn't used to startle him did now—it was hard to explain to someone who hadn't been in a battle. He liked to know where people were—exactly. He didn't like being snuck up on, and the pain meds were making him less able to hear the tiny sounds his soldier's training told him to listen for.

"I came in when Kaitlyn left." Apparently, she still felt like this house was her own, and frankly, he wasn't positive that it wouldn't be hers again. He couldn't see a marriage to Andy Granger lasting. "I wanted to talk to you about something."

"About what?" Brody asked.

"Andy."

Of course. What else? Brody had never had much of an issue with Andy Granger until the day he sold out to those moron land developers. Their big representative had swaggered around Hope wearing neon cowboy boots and a belt buckle the size of a dinner plate, and everyone had the good sense to steer clear, except Andy Granger. If it weren't for Andy's sellout, their crops wouldn't be failing and their ranch wouldn't be drying into dust.

"What about him?" Brody asked blandly.

"He's not as bad as you think," she said with a small smile.

"Apparently, he's convinced you of that," Brody retorted. What had Andy done on that cattle drive—brainwashed her? And the rest of the family, too, because they'd all been at the wedding.

"He had no idea what would happen to our land, Brody. You know that. He didn't have a crystal ball, and it was complicated."

"I doubt it was *that* complicated."

Dakota fiddled with her wedding ring—white gold and diamonds. At least Andy hadn't cheaped out on the jewelry.

"Which one of us will get the ranch when Mom and Dad go?" she asked.

This was an abrupt change of topic, and he eyed his sister curiously.

"You always wanted to run this place," he replied. Before she married Andy, that is. He'd thought they'd already agreed on that much. Had she changed her mind now that she'd joined the Grangers? Or was Andy angling to take over their land, too?

"But you're back now," she countered.

"Mom and Dad aren't exactly dying, are they?" There was no point in discussing all of this now. He wasn't planning on sticking around for the long term anyway, and six months from now, Dakota might have left Andy and be back home.

"But think about it," she pressed. "Dad doesn't have any cash tucked away. This ranch is the entire inheritance. So, yes, I always wanted to run this place, but what about you? When our father dies—and let's pray that's not for a long, long time—do you really want to be cut out of everything?"

"Of course not."

"So how would we split it?" she asked.

This wasn't something he wanted to talk about. He'd just had his best friend die in front of him, and he couldn't grapple with his parents' eventual passing right now. They'd figure something out, he was sure. He and Dakota had always been close, and he didn't for a second suspect that she'd try and steal his half of anything.

"Why are we talking about this?" he asked irritably.

"The point is," Dakota said, "that inheritances can be tricky. Andy and Chet had a ranch to split, and their father gave them each half the land."

"Sounds fair to me," Brody muttered.

"Except Chet was using Andy's land for pasture. In essence, Andy had nothing. He technically owned land that he couldn't do anything with."

"Then sell to his brother," Brody said. "That's what people do."

"The developers could give him twice as much as the land was worth," she said. "And he was faced with a chance to buy a business at the same time. He and Chet had this massive falling out, and Andy sold for twice as much money. If he'd sold to his brother, he'd still owe the bank for his business. He sold to the developers, and he owns his company free and clear."

"Your point?" Brody asked testily.

"I'm saying, Andy isn't as bad as you think. He

and Chet are trying to patch things up, but I can see how complicated one ranch and two heirs can make things."

"Tell you what, Dakota," Brody said with a small smile. "You have my promise that I won't do anything like that to you."

"Dad'll leave you the land, Brody," she said simply. "It doesn't matter what you and I agree to. Legally speaking, you're going to inherit."

"Maybe not," he said with a frown. He'd always known that his dad intended to leave the ranch to his son, but Dakota was the one who wanted it so badly she could taste it. When Brody up and left for the army, he was pretty sure his dad's plans would have changed, too.

"Give Andy a chance," she said quietly. "He's a good guy, and he's paying for our irrigation system."

"You sure about that?" Brody wasn't the kind of man who counted his chickens too early.

"The money is in my personal bank account," she said. "We'll start the installation this spring."

That surprised him. He'd expected Andy to make some big promises in order to win the Masons over, but he hadn't expected him to back it up with cash.

"Where did he get that kind of money?" he demanded.

"He's pretty good at making money," she said, and he caught the flicker of pleasure in her expression. "His car dealership in Billings is making a steady profit, and he's done some smart investing."

"Okay..." Brody said with a nod, although he felt

a twinge of discomfort. "I don't like taking that kind of cash, though."

"You aren't taking it," she said with a shrug. "I am. And he's my husband, so I don't feel badly at all. So you can stop worrying about that right now."

Brody rolled his eyes. She knew him too well, apparently. Sisters had a way of figuring out your buttons quicker than anyone else. A smile crept over Dakota's face and her eyes glowed in the soft flicker of the firelight.

"It's so strange to be over there...working the Granger land like it's my own." A guilty look crossed her face. "I worry about Dad over here. I mean, I still help him with a lot, and Chet has sent some ranch hands to pitch in, but it isn't the same."

"He'll hire more help," Brody said pragmatically. "Things will pick up."

"But you're back now." She fixed him with a pleading look.

And he was supposed to take up where he left off—ranching by his dad's side. It wasn't that he didn't love this land, and it wasn't that he didn't love this work, but he and his father had never seen eye-to-eye about anything from politics to animal husbandry.

"I see where you're going with this, Dakota, but Dad won't give an inch on this place. His land, his rules," Brody retorted. "So I'm supposed to act like a hired hand around here?"

"No, you're supposed to act like the guy who's going to run it after Dad's too old to do the work."

But even when his dad was too old to work, he

wouldn't be too old to complain, and that was part of what Brody had been so keen to escape. Working with his old man had never been part of the plan, no matter how much Brody loved ranching.

"Just think about it," Dakota said. "A lot has changed around here. It might be better than you think."

Was his sister right, or was she trying to appease her own conscience for getting married to the enemy next door?

"I've got to go work on a tractor," she said after a moment. "It's dripping oil something fierce. I'd better get out there."

Whose tractor—the Grangers' or their own? Maybe it didn't matter as much as he thought. That was his sister, all right, the little grease monkey. If she wasn't training horses, she was tinkering with engines. Andy had married a very able woman, but he was also getting a woman who could hold her own against an army if necessary. Granger might not know what he was in for, and that little thought was what made him smile to himself. Besides, she also had a big burly brother, who'd already knocked one guy around for treating her badly, and he'd be more than willing to do it again if Andy ever messed up.

He waved as she headed toward the kitchen and out the back door, leaving Brody in silence. The fire popped and the heat from the glowing wood felt good as it emanated against his bad leg.

They'd had a ranch hand who used to always sit with one hip toward the fire on cattle drives, and now Brody could understand that. He'd probably be doing the same thing from now on—taking advantage of heat to soothe away some aches and pains—because he couldn't imagine this leg ever being 100 percent again.

He pulled out Nina's envelope and looked down at the crinkled paper. It was addressed to him, care of Kaitlyn. She could have sent it to his house directly, but maybe she didn't trust that he'd receive it—he no longer knew what lengths his family would go to protect his feelings, as dumb as that was.

He slipped a finger in the corner and tore the envelope open. There was a single sheet of paper inside, and as he pulled it out, he could see Nina's back-slanted handwriting. She used to dot all her *i*'s with hearts when they were dating.

He could hear her voice in the words, and as his eyes flowed over the familiar script, he paused, the information sinking in and his anger simmering higher. This was the side of the story she hadn't told anyone, the side of the story she'd kept private. He was glad she'd told him, though. It might sting, but honesty was better.

Not a single heart-dotted *i*. She'd done him the favor of not signing her full married name—Nina Dickerson. That would have stung more, even though it was implied. She was sorry, but—it was very much over between them. Maybe he'd been tricking himself thinking that by putting a ring on her finger he'd stay in her mind. That was bitterness talking.

He tossed the letter toward the fire, and a draft caught it and set it lightly down on the other chair.

Blast. He was going to burn that letter if it was the last thing he did. He closed his eyes as he pushed past the pain and rose to his feet. His crutches were within reach, but right now, he didn't want to lean on them, he wanted to conquer something—anything!

He took a step forward, pain searing up from his thigh and into his groin, but he kept moving, thumping heavily back down onto his good leg. He couldn't put much weight on the bad leg for long, but he was most certainly making progress across the floor toward the other chair.

He clenched his teeth as he took another step, relieved to find that his head wasn't swimming the way it had this morning. Maybe it was the fresh medication in his system, but with a couple more steps, he reached the chair and bent just enough to grab the corner of the letter between two fingers. He tossed it toward the fire again, and this time it landed in the coals, and that back-slanted handwriting started to curl and blacken as the paper caught fire.

Standing there watching it burn, he glanced back at the chair he'd just vacated and realized that he'd walked about five feet on his own without any crutches. He felt a surge of victory. His victories seemed small these days, but he'd take them where he could find them. Kaitlyn would be impressed, too, he realized wryly. When was the last time he'd looked to impress a girl by walking five steps?

But he was a man who could endure pain and get

through it. He'd keep moving forward. That's what cowboys—and soldiers—did.

THE NEXT MORNING, as Kaitlyn bumped along the gravel road in the family pickup truck, her mind was on that letter. When she'd given it to him, she'd been relieved to relinquish responsibility and put it right back where it belonged—on Nina's shoulders—but things felt different with some time to think. They'd all spent so much emotional energy trying to protect Brody that it was hard to stop now that he was home again.

"Nina has a good heart," her father told her that morning. "Don't be too hard on her. At least they weren't married yet."

Her father had always gone easy on Nina, as if life for a knockout beauty was somehow harder than it was for the rest of them. But as a father, Ron Harpe erred on the side of tolerance. Kaitlyn was pretty sure he still thought of Nina as a girl in pigtails—whether that was good for his daughter or not.

"We were going to keep the secret until he got back," her father reminded her. "And now he's back. He's a grown man, sweetheart. Quit babying him."

Her father had a point, but despite those bulging muscles and steely gaze, Brody was still fragile. He'd been through a lot. He'd nearly died out there, and he'd had some ugly surprises upon returning home. Her father saw the grown man, but she saw the vulnerable war vet. She could only hope she hadn't made things worse. Nina's conscience could have waited, for all Kaitlyn was concerned, but the deed was done.

Kaitlyn pulled up the drive and parked. When she arrived at the side door, she found the screen shut but the main door open and Mrs. Mason pulling on her gum boots. She tugged a hand through her graying frizzy hair and reached for a pair of work gloves.

"Good morning," Kaitlyn said.

"Morning. I'm just heading out to check on a sick cow. Sorry for the rush." She shot Kaitlyn a smile. Millie Mason was looking decidedly more relaxed now that her son was back from Afghanistan, and her eyes had a new sparkle. None of this had been ideal, but one mother's heart was very full.

"No problem." Kaitlyn stood back as the older woman pushed open the screen and slipped past her onto the step. The air outside was cold, and the snow had a thick crust over it.

"Your patient is already up, too," Millie said with a smile. "You'll see! Oh, and I didn't get breakfast made, so…"

So it would be on Kaitlyn to feed Brody. That wasn't a big deal. Unlike Nina, Kaitlyn knew how to cook. She waved to Millie, then stepped into the warmth inside. She started when she saw Brody standing at the fridge. He had only one crutch tucked under his arm, and he glanced back at her with a slightly smug look on his face.

"Look at you!" she exclaimed, pulling off her gloves and jacket. "How much is this hurting?"

"Like hell," Brody said with a tight smile. "But it's worth it. I'm making breakfast. What do you want?"

"I don't want you landing in my breakfast," she said with a roll of her eyes. "I'll get it."

"Have I shown off enough?" he asked, then hobbled toward the table and sank into a chair. He looked a little wan, the pain probably near unbearable levels, but he was trying—really trying—and she felt a wave of tenderness. The same old Brody. That was why it was so easy to fall for him. He was so strong and sweet, but with a core of steel. Brody never gave up—not once he was focused on something...or someone. Kaitlyn had never been lucky enough to garner his focus.

"Very impressive. Now stay down." She opened the fridge, her gaze falling on a bowl of different-sized fresh eggs on the second shelf. They'd be from the Masons' chickens out back. "How about eggs?"

"Sure." Brody twisted around, his dark gaze following her as she moved about the kitchen. Heat rose in her face at his scrutiny.

"Have you taken any new pain meds this morning?" she asked by way of distracting him. "Keep in mind that I count the pills."

Brody arched an eyebrow. "You think I'd lie to you?"

No, she didn't. Brody had always been the honorable type, but pain medication addiction was relatively common for injuries this severe, and Brody's pain wasn't only physical. He'd been through the wringer since he got back—and she also felt more in control as the nurse than she did as the friend.

"Any new pain meds?" she repeated, shooting him a no-nonsense look.

"No, ma'am," he replied with a teasing smile. "You've gotten bossier."

If she didn't look at him, if she just listened to the tone of his voice and the silly banter, it was possible to imagine that no time had passed, and that Brody was the same muscle-bound cowboy he'd always been.

"No, I haven't." She cracked four eggs into a bowl and started to whisk them together into a creamy froth. "I just have reason to focus it all on you. Aren't you lucky?"

Brody rewarded her with a chuckle.

"Look, Brody, I felt a little bad about dumping that letter on you."

"I read it."

She glanced back to find his gaze still focused on her. He raised an eyebrow.

"Curious as to what she said?"

"Yes," she admitted.

"Brian got her pregnant."

It took a moment for his words to sink in, and when they did, Kaitlyn frowned. "What?"

"And she's very sorry, and all that," Brody said drily. "Awfully apologetic. And pregnant."

Pregnant! That would explain the quick wedding. They'd all begged them to hold off and wait a little bit, but Nina wouldn't hear of it. She was getting married immediately, and everyone had to scramble to try and keep the news as quiet as possible, and to call everyone who had any immediate knowledge to warn them from letting Brody know. If Nina had just waited, it would have been so much less complicated, but now she understood the pressure.

"Wow." Kaitlyn shook her head slowly. "She didn't tell me."

"She said she hadn't told anyone yet," Brody said. "But I'm in no mood to keep secrets. There've been enough of those."

"How far along is she?" Kaitlyn asked.

"She said she's due in May."

Kaitlyn did the mental math... Nina was five months pregnant? But then, she hadn't seen her sister since the wedding.

"Brody, I'm so sorry." She didn't know what else to say.

"For what?" he asked bitterly. "You didn't do it."

She knew that, but she could only imagine how much this would hurt Brody. His fiancée and his best friend were having a baby together.

"You deserve better."

She meant that more deeply than Brody probably knew. She hadn't blamed him for falling in love with her sister, because everyone did eventually. Nina was gorgeous. One look at her, and men's minds scrambled like farm-fresh eggs. So if he'd wanted to devote his life to a beautiful wife, she couldn't blame him, but he deserved someone who would make him a birthday cake, even if it tasted terrible—and with Nina's cooking, it most certainly would. He deserved someone who'd be excited enough to go out with him that she'd be at least close to ready by the time he arrived to pick her up, instead of leaving him in the kitchen for an hour with her nonthreatening younger sister. And at the very least, he deserved someone who would wait for him while he fought overseas.

"Ever wonder what their childhood Valentines would have said?" he asked bitterly. "Maybe they'd be the secret Valentines—the little girl in a short dress with her finger to her lips. Shh."

Their old game had taken on a sadder, more bitter tone, and she didn't know how to answer that. A couple of beats of silence stretched between them.

"I want to go see my horse today," Brody said, then jutted his chin toward the stove. "That pan's hot."

Kaitlyn startled when she saw the smoking pan. She dropped a pat of butter into the center and swirled it around. She was still stunned by the news of her sister's pregnancy, but Brody seemed to be off it already...and he wanted to go to the barn.

"The barn is pretty far," she said.

"You can drive me."

"You're making really great progress," she said, dumping the egg mixture into the pan with a sizzle. Then she looked back at him. "But that's still a long way out. If you're in pain, a bumpy ride on a dirt road is going to be agony."

Brody looked away, toward the kitchen window, and for a moment she thought he'd accepted her point. Why would he want to put himself through that? Did Nina's confession have anything to do with this?

"I'll put it this way," he said slowly. "I'm going to the barn today. You can come along if you want."

Kaitlyn blinked. So that's the way it was going to be.

"And if you faint?" she asked pointedly.

"Men don't faint," he said. "We might slip in and out of consciousness, but it's in a very manly way."

Kaitlyn shook her head, ignoring his deadpan humor. "That's very cute until I have to try and catch you and slip a disc or something."

"I won't faint."

He couldn't actually promise that, especially in his condition.

"If I refuse to drive you?" she asked.

"I'll walk."

She had a feeling he'd do just that. She pictured him hobbling down the gravel road toward the barn, then keeling over into the ditch. A body could only endure so much pain before it shut down. She didn't have much of a choice.

"I'll drive you under protest," she said, then sighed and flipped the omelet in half. "But if you faint, I'm letting you drop like a sack of potatoes."

A small smile turned up one side of his mouth. "I'd expect nothing less."

Chapter Four

A half hour later, their breakfast was done and Brody leaned on a crutch and on Kaitlyn's shoulder as he made his way down the steps from the back door. The pain was intense, and every time his good foot hit the ground, no matter how gently he tried to land, the agony blazed up his wounded leg and his stomach roiled. He paused to breathe.

"Changed your mind?" Kaitlyn asked, sounding a little more hopeful than he liked.

"No," he grunted.

Truthfully, had his nurse been anyone else, he would have turned back and crawled into the house like the failure he was, but not in front of Kaitlyn. She was different—more than a nurse—and her opinion of him mattered more than he cared to admit right now. She'd called him brave, jokingly or not, and he'd vowed to live up to that.

"Okay, one last step," she said.

There were only three. He held his breath as he came down the last step and let it out in a rush as the pain radiated through his leg once more. But they were done with the stairs. He noticed the worried look on her face, and felt the way her grip on his arm tightened.

"I'm fine," he said. "Who's driving?"

She cracked a smile at last, a sparkle of amusement entering those big dark eyes, and she shook her head. "Funny. I'm driving."

He was gratified to see her smile, and he liked the way her cheeks tinged pink. He hated being the patient, the powerless one on his back. If he could make her laugh, then they'd be a step closer to the old dynamic where she'd laugh and roll her eyes at him when he teased her.

He'd liked that—the way she'd never taken him entirely seriously. But it was sweeter when he'd been her future brother-in-law, and he'd been strong and tough and fun. Now, what was he? Wounded, broken, cast aside. And he probably needed to be taken seriously more than ever before.

That morning he'd gotten a phone call from an old buddy in Hope, and after a stilted conversation, they'd hung up. No offer to get together. Just plain old duty—you'd better call the guy who went to war, or you'll look like a jerk. There had been a few phone calls like that since he'd gotten back, and he could feel the distance in their tones. It wasn't only family who saw him differently, it was the whole town.

Kaitlyn opened the passenger side door of the old Chevy farm truck. It was rusted and dented, and probably the toughest old dinosaur around. It might not be pretty, but it was reliable. Brody eased himself up into the seat, stifling a grimace.

"Deep breaths," she said quietly, and she put a supporting hand under his thigh as he lifted his leg into the cab. She thought she was helping, but that was only making matters worse. This would be so much easier if she looked more like her aunt Bernice.

"I'm good, I'm good," he said as he settled his boot onto the floor of the truck. "Let's go."

She slammed his door shut, and for a moment he sat in silence as she circled around to the driver's side. It felt good to be in a pickup again. It would feel better to be in the driver's seat, but that would have to wait. This was a good first step. He needed to get out to the barn and smell the hay and the horses. He needed to have a good heart-to-heart with Champ. The old boy would probably be resentful about his lengthy absence, but Brody needed this just as much as Champ did. A homecoming wasn't complete until he connected with his favorite horse.

Kaitlyn got up into the driver's side and cast him a sidelong look as she turned the key and the truck rumbled to life.

"So, any boyfriends I should be vetting for you?" Brody asked.

"Not at the moment." She put the truck into gear and eased forward. "I was so busy with studying and finishing up a semester early, that I haven't really had the time."

Good. Why did he like the idea of her being single? Probably just him being all big brotherly, but he had to admit that the feelings coursing through him when Kaitlyn leaned close to help him into a more comfortable position, or when she helped peel his clothes off that first night…those feelings weren't brotherly in the least. He'd chalked it up to a natural male response to a beautiful woman. Because Kaitlyn had certainly blossomed over the last year, and she'd gone from kid sister to…well, a whole lot less "kid sister."

He glanced over at her, those auburn waves tumbling around her shoulders, setting off her creamy complexion in the watery morning sunlight. Not that it should matter to him. She'd also been capable of effortlessly deceiving him for months on end. He'd best keep that in mind.

"So, what was the wedding like?" Brody asked.

Kaitlyn didn't answer for a moment, steering around a pothole in the gravel drive that led down toward the barn. The rumble of the motor and the icy bumps on the road made him ache in new places.

"It was small," she said at last.

He nodded. It wasn't like he really wanted to know the details of "the big day," even if he was curious. He'd asked his sister to help Nina put together a small wedding because his fiancée had seemed nervous. He'd assumed her nerves had been about wedding planning. How wrong could a guy get?

"You don't really want to hear about this, do you?" Kaitlyn looked over at him, her expression pained. "It wasn't a big, happy day. It was small. It was secret. And those of us who knew about it weren't feeling terribly supportive."

"Sounds awkward."

Nina had always maintained some pretty big expectations about her wedding day—something she'd made very clear to him, including the size of the diamond she would wear on her finger. Had she maintained those demands with Brian?

"I don't know…" Kaitlyn sighed, then shot him an apologetic look as they went over a bump. "Sorry. That one was big… Nina has always been rather spoiled. She got her way all the time. You were probably the worst, you know."

He winced in pain, then shot her an exasperated look. "Are you seriously blaming me for this one?" he demanded.

They were nearing the barn, and she put the truck into a lower gear.

"I didn't say that." She gripped the steering wheel tighter, irritation glimmering in her eyes, which were fixed on the drive ahead of them. "But you were just as bad as everyone else. Whatever she wanted, you gave her. And you never stopped to question anything. She took two hours to get ready to go out, and you just sat around with me, playing cards. Why didn't you tell her to hurry up? Why did you just take that?"

Was Kaitlyn seriously expecting him to holler up the stairs at his girlfriend? He wasn't that kind of guy. There'd be no Ricky Ricardo "You've got some 'splaining to do, Lucy" from him.

She eased the truck to a stop and turned on him. She was ticked off, that was obvious enough. What had he done now? Apparently, he didn't know women as well as he thought.

"You were good company," he said with a cajoling smile. "Besides, I'm not the kind of guy who orders around his woman."

"Not good enough," she retorted. "You could have talked to her privately and told her how it made you feel—"

"How do you know I didn't?"

He'd mentioned it to Nina a few times. Not that he didn't like to chat with Kaitlyn, but she was right—it showed where Nina's priorities lay. Nina hadn't taken his concerns seriously, though, and Brody had figured it was the price of being with a beautiful woman. Apparently, Nina's smoky eyes and perfectly fitting outfits took some time. And the other guys thought he was downright lucky to be with her. But, yeah… it bugged him.

"If you did, she didn't take you too seriously." She shot him a knowing look, and he resented how much she could read into the things he didn't say. "You knew what she was, Brody. You knew that she cared more about her makeup regime than your feelings. You seemed okay with that. You knew that she didn't care enough about your birthday to even try her hand at making a boxed cake!"

Brody felt his smile slip. She was right—he'd known that Nina was self-centered, but somehow he'd thought with a family like hers, they'd get through all right. They said that you weren't just marrying a girl, you were marrying the whole family. Well, with the Harpes, that was a good thing.

"So I should have realized she'd never wait for me?" he demanded.

"Yes!" Kaitlyn tugged a hand through her hair. "Look—what she did was wrong. None of us agreed with her, but you actually thought she'd get stronger and more resilient with you gone?"

A year had made a big difference in the rest of them. Was personal growth such an impossibility to expect from Nina? Maybe it had been, but a year had done something to Kaitlyn that he couldn't quite explain. She'd gotten a whole lot stronger.

"You did," he said.

Kaitlyn blinked, opened her mouth to say something, then clamped it shut again. He'd surprised her with that, but it was the truth.

"I thought with you there..." Brody tried to explain. "I thought you'd be able to give her a few words of wisdom if she needed them."

"She needed more than words." Bitterness tinged her tone.

"I thought if I gave her a ring, a wedding to look forward to—" He didn't finish the thought. He'd given her everything he could, but it hadn't mattered. The ring hadn't been enough, and neither had her family.

"You weren't the only one who put up with Nina's crap," Kaitlyn said after a moment. "I made excuses for her, too. But at the end of the day, a woman either stands on her own two feet, or she doesn't."

Brody was silent. She was right, of course. He'd

been leaving for Afghanistan, and he'd been scared. Proposing was life affirming. It cemented in his own heart that he needed to come back in one piece.

"And she never told me," Kaitlyn added. "I had no idea she and Brian had started anything, so I didn't have a chance to give her any words of wisdom, as you put it. Your sister caught them making out in the movie theater, and that was the first I knew of it."

He winced. Dakota had already told him the story—it was tacky, and incredibly beneath Nina, in his opinion.

"Well, it is what it is," he said. "I'd better get used to it."

That was all he had left, really. There was no saving face in this. Nina and Brian were married and expecting a baby, and that ended it. He reached for the door handle. "I'm going to go get reacquainted with Champ."

Kaitlyn came around and helped him down. She handed him his crutches and he took his first swinging steps toward the barn door.

When he was being flown back to American soil, he'd known that he'd changed, and he'd been counting on a woman to tell him who he was again. She hadn't been the perfect woman. Kaitlyn had been right about that—he'd known her shortcomings, and he'd put up with her slights. He'd just hoped that when he got back again, having a high maintenance fiancée would snap him back into his old self. Nina wouldn't have tolerated anything else.

But now he doubted that would have worked. He'd

changed, and he didn't have the patience for two-hour waits on Nina anymore. They would have fought, and he would have started asking more of Nina, just as Kaitlyn thought he should have ages ago, and he and Nina would have broken up. Because Nina wasn't interested in giving anything more. She expected the world on a platter in exchange for her beautiful self. That was the silent agreement, and he'd signed on like an idiot. At least a breakup at this point would have been a choice they'd made together instead of a gut-wrenching surprise. In the end, though, he hadn't had the choice. The breakup, however, had been on its way from the day he proposed. And maybe Kaitlyn was right—he should have seen it coming.

KAITLYN GOT BRODY settled on a couple bales of hay. It wasn't fair to be mad at Brody. She'd been very clearly angry with her sister this whole time, but this morning that pendulum had swung. Sheltering someone who didn't want her protection was hard work, and after a while it got to chafing. Brody had proposed to the wrong woman, and he should have been smart enough to know that. Nina wanted to spend her life being beautiful and bubble-wrapped, and frankly, Brody wasn't going to get that luxury. He was a normal person, just like the rest of them, and Bubble Wrap wasn't an option.

She knew that her anger at her patient wasn't professional or entirely fair, but it was there, no matter how carefully she tried to tamp it out. The handsome cowboy still made her heart lurch as he looked up at his horse, and she heaved a sigh.

Champ was a bay gelding. He was a good horse—patient and intuitive—and that had a lot to do with Brody's training. The Masons were known for their horse training, and while Dakota had a reputation of being a Horse Whisperer, Brody had an innate talent with them, too. So what made him so blinded by a woman?

"It's been a while, Champ," Brody said quietly. "I missed you, fella."

Champ nickered and bent his head toward his master. Brody stroked his nose, and it seemed to Kaitlyn that Champ sensed his master's wounded status, because he came right up against the rails and then dropped his head over Brody's shoulder in a full body hug. Brody leaned his head against the horse's muscular neck. Tears misted Kaitlyn's eyes, and she looked away. Why did men have to be so stupid and endearing at the same time?

She felt as if she were intruding on this unspoken communication between a man and his horse. She opened her mouth to say that she'd be back, but then she decided against it and silently headed outside.

Kaitlyn squinted and sucked in a chestful of brisk winter air. Snow capped the fence posts, and sunlight sparkled on the stretches of snowfall that remained untouched. Dirt-crusted tracks led around the barn, where workers passed, and she looked back up the road that led toward the house, hidden behind a swell of snow. Out here at the barn, it was easy to imagine that they were alone.

She needed some space to herself just as much as Brody seemed to. Before agreeing to this job, she'd promised herself that she'd be careful. This wasn't just a nursing position. And Brody wasn't just an old friend, either…he was the guy she'd measured all the others against. If she'd had any other moral option, she would have declined, but they needed a nurse, and she needed to atone for her own role in this mess, so here she was, and she kept galloping past the lines she'd drawn for herself. She'd sworn that she'd be professional and controlled, but the minute he said something that annoyed her, all those reserves had been forgotten and all her opinions came out in a flood.

She shouldn't have said that in the truck. She was already kicking herself for it.

I'm his nurse, she reminded herself. *Keep it professional.*

Which was easier said than done with their lengthy history. But he hadn't been talking to her as his nurse, he'd been talking to his friend. And regardless of secrets kept, Kaitlyn had always been his loyal friend.

One of her carefully kept secrets was how much she'd longed for something more with Brody—for him to look up one day and realize that he knew her better than he knew her sister. But even if he realized that, it wouldn't mean that he'd want the same kind of relationship that she did.

It wasn't Brody's good looks, either. He was tall, muscular and had the most playful eyes—or at least he used to. His laid-back jocularity had hidden a deeper sensitivity that Nina had never recognized. Not that it was Kaitlyn's business to address his deeper sensitivities—certainly not back then. Kaitlyn had no wish to cross any lines with her sister's fiancé, and she'd curbed those feelings as firmly as she knew how. Brody had made his choice, and Kaitlyn had been willing to live with that choice. But when he seemed surprised that Nina hadn't been his rock under pressure, that had been too much.

Stupid man. You should have known!

"Hey, there..."

Kaitlyn looked over in surprise to see a ranch hand eyeing her from a few paces off. He was gangly and tall with tobacco-stained teeth and a sparse beard. His gaze flickered up and down her unapologetically.

"Morning." She looked away, hoping he'd move on, but he didn't. He took a step closer and cocked his head to one side.

"I'm new here. Still getting to know everyone." He managed to make those words sound suggestive and she shot him an annoyed look. Some men still hadn't learned that leering wasn't a compliment. "I'm Nick, by the way."

"Don't let me keep you from your work," she said.

"Don't worry about me." A smile crept across his face. "I've got time."

The truck was a few yards away, and Kaitlyn did a quick scan of the area. She couldn't see any other workers. The ranch hand seemed to come to the same conclusion, because he closed the distance between them, his tongue moving over his lips. He stopped a little too close to her, and his breath smelled of stale cigarettes and not enough brushing. She turned her face away.

"I always liked a redhead," he said with a low laugh.

Her hair was auburn, not red, but she doubted that this guy cared about such distinctions. Kaitlyn hated giving ground because it made her look weak, but his breath was nauseating and she took a step back. He followed her in a smooth movement that made her retreat useless.

"Leave me alone," she said pointedly. "I'm not interested."

"You don't know me," he responded. "You'll like me when you know me better. What's your name?"

He reached out and fingered a lock of her hair, and she swatted her hair back over her shoulder. He dropped his hand and that hungry, flirtatious look turned slightly meaner.

"Stop it," she snapped, and in that moment, she saw her challenge reflected in those gray-flecked eyes. This ranch hand—Nick—wasn't going to back down until she kneed him in the groin. It was unfortunate that he'd gamble with his ability to father children like this, but—

"She said to leave her alone." Brody's bass rumble came from the barn, and Kaitlyn looked over at him with a wave of relief. He filled the doorway, and even stooped slightly over his crutches, he was an intimidatingly large man. Brody's black gaze was directed at the ranch hand.

"Just saying hello," Nick said tersely. "It's a free country."

"A country I fought for," Brody growled, and he took two swinging steps forward with his crutches. "Don't lecture me about freedoms, cowboy. And trust me, I've got what it takes to bring you down from here. I suggest you back off."

Brody's gaze had changed to something Kaitlyn had never seen before—steely, laser sharp and controlled. It was the soldier shining through, the military-trained efficiency that turned a cowboy into something more. The ranch hand muttered a curse, spat on the ground and sauntered off, and as Brody watched him go, that drilling gaze morphed into an expression of mild disappointment.

He wanted to take him down.

That realization hit Kaitlyn like a hoof to the stomach. The army had changed him more than she'd realized. The Brody she'd known had been strong and dependable, but he hadn't been quite so...dangerous. She'd expected him to be dealing with some PTSD from the trauma, but she hadn't expected the changes to be so deep. When Brody turned back toward her, his eyes were soft and familiar again, the soldier in him buried once more.

"You okay?" he asked.

"I'm fine." She nodded quickly. "Are you?"

Brody winced as he took another hop toward her

and then glanced in the direction the ranch hand had disappeared behind the barn.

"He scared you," he said simply, ignoring her question.

"Yeah," she admitted. He'd had the look of a man who took what he wanted, regardless of a woman's interest, but Brody had scared her a little bit, too.

"I'll fire him," Brody said. "I don't want a guy like that around here."

"Can you do that?" Kaitlyn asked, squinting up at him. Mr. Mason had always kept a pretty firm hand on the running of this ranch. He was a man who wouldn't retire gracefully.

"Yeah, well..." Brody shrugged, a small smile playing at the corners of his lips. "I'm back now, aren't I? Trust me. He'll be gone by morning."

He was back. Did that mean he'd stay? She pushed down any lingering hopes she'd indulged about that.

"What is your pain level?" she asked, bringing the conversation back to the job she was hired to do.

"It's pretty bad."

"You need rest." She nodded toward the truck. "Let's head back."

He must have been in a considerable amount of pain, because this time he didn't even bother putting up a fight. When he was settled in the passenger seat of the old Chevy, she noticed his steely, controlled gaze move slowly over the barn like the sweep of crosshairs. She looked over her shoulder and saw no one.

Brody had left this ranch a cowboy, and he'd returned a soldier. She wondered if he'd ever be able to look at a field the same way again, or if he'd earned a lifetime of sweeping perimeters for an enemy locked in his memory.

She headed around to the driver's side of the vehicle and shivered.

I'm his nurse, she reminded herself. And that mattered more when she realized what Brody was dealing with. Whether he realized it or not, he needed her for a whole lot more than a wounded leg.

Chapter Five

That evening Brody sat at the kitchen table, watching his father scarf down a roast beef sandwich. Ken Mason was a solid man with a weather-reddened face and iron gray hair that stood up from his head as if he'd had a bad fright. He ate like he did most things— in silence.

Brody chewed the last bite of his own sandwich and glanced at the clock. Kaitlyn would arrive in the next hour to help him with his leg, but he'd been thinking of her ever since she'd left that afternoon. He hadn't liked the way that ranch hand had been moving in on her, and her tone of voice had been fierce and slightly scared. The thought of that man laying one unwanted finger on her brought back his army training like a jolt of electricity.

Had Nick tried anything after Brody's warning, he wasn't sure what he would have done, and that scared him a little. He wasn't in Afghanistan now. The kind of force he was trained to use wasn't justified here on the ranch. He knew that, and it would have taken all of his self-restraint to rein himself in.

Luckily, Nick had taken the warning.

Brody's mother opened the back door and came clomping into the house. She wore a quilted jacket and a pair of loose pants tucked into tall rubber boots.

"Don't fill up!" she said, glancing toward them at the table. "I'm making a chicken for dinner."

This was the image of his mom that he'd held on to through the years—and she hadn't changed much since he was a kid. A bit grayer, maybe, and a few more lines around her eyes, but that smile was the same, and so were her protective boundaries when it came to their appetites for dinner.

"I'll have room," Ken said with a half smile cast in the direction of his wife. "I'm going back out to check on the herd after dinner, though. We've got a heifer that's limping."

"I wanted to talk to you about something first," Brody said, and his father raised his bushy eyebrows.

"What about?"

"That ranch hand—Nick Something. He needs to go."

"Out of the question." Ken frowned and put down the last of his sandwich. "It's Nick Sutton, and he's got a real intuition when it comes to the cattle. He's a good worker—he's the one who pointed out the lame cow. Do you know how long it's been since I've had a ranch hand I could rely on?"

"He's a creep." An image of Nick leaning hungrily over Kaitlyn rose in his mind, and the anger came with it. It didn't matter how good he was with the cattle if he couldn't be trusted around a woman.

"Well, you'll have to man up if he makes you uncomfortable," his father chuckled.

Anger sparked in Brody's chest. He was army trained. If anyone should be nervous, it was Nick, because without some serious self-restraint, old Nick would have been in need of some round-the-clock nursing of his own.

"It isn't me. It's Kaitlyn."

"What was she doing with Nick?" Ken asked with a frown. "She's your nurse. She isn't supposed to be wandering the ranch."

"She was with me," Brody replied. "And Nick wasn't taking no for an answer."

"Well, I'm saying no. Nick Sutton stays."

This was the way it had always been—his father's word was law around here. Ken didn't follow anything but his own gut when it came to the running of this ranch, and so far he'd done just fine for himself. But not for Brody.

"How are you feeling, dear?" his mother asked, running a hand across Brody's shoulder on her way past.

"I'm fine, Mom." He tried not to let his annoyance show. "Dad, I'm serious. What if it had been Dakota? What then?"

As if on cue, a truck's engine rumbled into the drive. It was probably Dakota come back from the fields.

"She's never mentioned him to me," his father replied. "And if he'd been a problem, she would have. You know your sister."

He did know his sister, and it looked like his father had started to rely on Dakota's instincts over the last year. She'd always been fighting for him to take her seriously, and it looked like Brody's time away had changed that dynamic.

"All right," Brody said slowly. "Here's the thing. I'm going to inherit this ranch when you're gone, aren't I?"

"Eventually," his father said. "But I'm not exactly wilting away yet, my boy."

"Ken..." Brody's mother's voice cut through the room, and she dropped a fresh chicken into a roasting pan with a rattle. "If you want to work with your son, you'd better let him have some input. If he's man enough to fight for our country, drink and vote, then I think he's man enough to make a few of these calls."

Ken was silent, and it was obvious that Brody's parents had discussed this at some point, because his mother didn't say anything else. She turned back to the fridge and Brody's father chewed on the side of his cheek.

"Fine. This time, we'll do it your way. I'll fire him, but I'm giving him a reference."

The concession was the best that Brody would get, even if the reference suggested that Brody was somehow being unfair in the ranch hand's treatment. The side door opened and Dakota came inside, Andy Granger behind her.

"Dakota," Ken said. "Do you know that new ranch hand—Nick?"

"Sure." She bent to slip off her boots.

"What do you think of him?" their father asked gruffly.

Dakota undid her coat. "He's a creep. Why?"

Ken sighed, and Andy raised an eyebrow questioningly. This wasn't Andy's domain, and Brody wasn't about to invite him into the discussion.

"It's already settled," Brody said with a sigh. "He's being let go."

Dakota didn't seem to care a great deal about the ranch hand's fate. She and Andy were exchanging private smiles as Andy took off his jacket. They were in love—as irritating as that was to watch.

"Mom invited us for dinner," Dakota said.

Dakota gave Andy's hand a squeeze then crossed the kitchen to talk to her mother. Brody cut a glance toward his brother-in-law. They were related now, and Brody wasn't used to this yet. The webcammed wedding hadn't seemed real somehow, but being back home with Andy sauntering through his kitchen— that was real.

"Glad you're back," Andy said, putting a hand out. Brody grudgingly shook hands with him.

Ken had settled back into his habitual silence, sipping a cup of coffee. Brody had won this round with his old man, hadn't he? They'd always butted heads like this—his father holding the line like a stubborn bull. Ken Mason didn't bend for anyone except his wife, and frankly, Brody was tired of having to go through his mother to get his father to see any sense.

Andy sat in a chair opposite him, and Brody

pushed his empty plate away. "So how's married life?" Brody asked.

"Blissful." Andy grinned in Dakota's direction.

"You sure marriage will suit you?" Brody asked. "That's one woman for the rest of your life, you know."

Andy had a bit of a reputation for being a ladies' man, and Brody didn't think the clarification was off base. Andy had to convince her family now, and Brody wasn't as easily swayed by sweet talk and kisses. At least not from Andy.

"Brody!" Dakota retorted from across the kitchen. "Leave him alone!"

Brody rolled his eyes. Yeah, the poor helpless cowboy. He *was* irritated, but he couldn't fairly blame Andy for it, either. It was all of them—he was back at the family home again, and while he was supposed to feel safe here, he didn't. That's what Home had meant to all of the boys overseas…all those old feelings of belonging and security. That's what he and the other soldiers overseas had talked about—how great it would be to get home again and be with their families, how great it would be not to have to sleep with a gun.

Except he missed the gun. He found himself reaching for it in the night and his hand closing over nothing but pillow. He always woke with a start when he couldn't find it.

"I'm not that kind of guy anymore," Andy said. "I know I'll have to prove it to you, but I'll treat her right. You'll see."

Brody didn't answer. Dakota was her own woman, and she'd married the man she wanted to marry, so Brody knew exactly how far his opinion went. Besides, much as he hated to admit it, Andy was proving to be moderately civilized.

"Well," his father said, pushing his coffee cup aside. "I'm going to check on that cow. I'll be back for that chicken dinner."

"You firing Nick tonight, or waiting until morning?" Brody asked. He wanted this nailed down.

"In the morning," his father replied. "I said I'd do it. Trust me."

Trust him. The words echoed inside of him. How could Brody trust any of them? That was the problem— the big, unspoken issue everyone had been dancing around since he got back. Everyone was acting like life was the same as it had always been, but nothing was the same.

Brody used to feel safe at home, and he no longer did. He used to like the feeling of wide-open spaces, and now the fence posts made his shoulder blades tingle. He used to take his ornery old father at his word, and he couldn't do that anymore. That wasn't only because of the lie—it was because of the war and the things he'd seen, too. Humanity was capable of brutal, terrible acts, and civilian ignorance truly was bliss. So he'd seen all of that and parts of him had broken that just weren't going to heal up again. A man couldn't witness that kind of destruction and go back to feeling safe on this planet. His sense of security was officially blown. And to top off that mangled mess, he'd discovered that they'd all lied to him. It was the last straw. Some of the burdens he carried had been unavoidable, like seeing his best friends die, but the deception from home hadn't been necessary. It was just...cruel.

"I did trust you, Dad," Brody said, his tone quiet but carrying. "I trusted all of you."

Silence descended onto the room, and Andy looked away uncomfortably. But if he wanted to be part of this family, he'd better be able to deal with the uncomfortable parts, too. Maybe Andy should know that he'd married into some of the most accomplished liars in the county.

Emotion choked off Brody's throat, and he swallowed with difficulty. Jeff had trusted him with his life, and he'd been blown to bits. So had Steve, and Raj. All three men had saved his hide more times than he could count, and all three were dead.

I've got your back. That's what they'd say when they lifted a rifle and got their eye level with the scope. *I've got your back, man.* That meant something in the army. You spoke the truth, or you shut your trap. Anything else was a waste of words. So how come his family felt so comfortable writing him lengthy letters and reassuring him that all was just as he'd left it when that was the furthest thing from the truth?

"You mean Nina?" his father said, shaking his head. "Brody, we explained—"

"Yeah, you did." Brody had been holding this in since his arrival, and the words came out before he could think better of them. "But here's the thing— when you're in the desert, you learn what it means to count on someone. My army buddies had my back every time I even went to the latrine. We said what we meant. No games. Who had time for games? And they could count on the fact that I'd rain down bullets to get them back safe. That's the kind of loyalty I learned in the army. Then I got home and—"

He didn't finish. They all knew what he'd come home to.

"We did what we thought we had to," his mother said, her voice shaking. "That was us raining down bullets for you, son! Do you think it was easy?"

"I trusted those guys with my life," he said huskily. "So you ask me to trust you, and I'm telling you that I don't think that's possible anymore."

"Son..." His mother's chin quivered with suppressed tears, and he felt a stab of guilt. He hated making her cry. His sister watched him warily, and his father just looked at that empty coffee mug. They'd disappointed him, but he could tell that he'd done the same to them. He wasn't the kind of returning hero they'd expected. Some homecoming this had turned out to be.

Then the back door opened again, and in stepped Kaitlyn. She stood there in the doorway, cold air whipping into the kitchen. She seemed to assess the scene pretty quickly, because her expression changed from one of cheerful greeting to caution. She shut the door behind her and glanced around. She was a part of this mess, but somehow, she was comforting, too.

He hated those kinds of uncomfortable tangles in his emotions. Why couldn't anything just stay simple and unsullied?

"I could come back—" she began.

"No," Brody grunted and used his good leg to push back his chair. "There's nothing else to say."

His chair fell backward with a clatter as he pushed himself painfully to his feet, and all eyes stayed riveted to him as he grabbed his crutches and heaved himself toward the sitting room. All eyes, that is, but Andy's. Andy was staring hard at the table top. And ironically enough, Andy was the only person in that room who hadn't lied to him. Yet.

THE MASONS LOOKED DEFLATED—all of them. Mrs. Mason wiped tears from her cheeks with the palms of her hand, and Mr. Mason stared vacantly in the direction his son had gone. Dakota gave Kaitlyn a wan smile. Andy Granger sat at the table, but she couldn't see his face.

"Sorry," Kaitlyn said. "Bad timing, I guess."

"It's okay," Mrs. Mason said. "Go on through."

Kaitlyn hung her coat on a hook and headed toward the next room. Their quiet voices started up behind her once she'd entered the sitting room, and she saw Brody standing by the front window, staring out at the yard. If it weren't for the army buzz cut and the crutches leaning against the window frame, it would be like no time had passed at all, and seeing him just standing there made her heart squeeze almost painfully.

She'd missed him…so much more than she'd ever let herself admit to. She'd spent the last year telling herself that Brody was Nina's fiancé, and she needed to keep her emotional distance. Then she'd spent the last couple of months trying to find ways to protect Brody from her sister's choices, and that had a way of tying up her emotions, too. So now that he was home and her job was so much smaller—just his medical care—all those feelings she'd been holding back and deflecting came in a flood.

But Nina had been his first choice, and if she'd stayed true, they'd be getting married in the next few weeks. She needed to hold on to that, because it was a fact.

Kaitlyn had just had a rather tense phone conversation with her sister. Kaitlyn had called to ask about her pregnancy, and Nina had responded the exact way Kaitlyn expected: she'd been overjoyed that she could finally talk about it, and she'd gushed about her cravings for KFC and talked about how fun it was to finally shop for maternity wear. Nina was pregnant, and Kaitlyn didn't begrudge her relishing this, but Nina hadn't seemed to save a thought for what was happening back in Hope.

And even more frustrating were Kaitlyn's own feelings—she was going to be an aunt! Nina would have a baby, and Kaitlyn would have a little niece or nephew to love and cuddle. Her loyalties were certainly divided, but babies were blessings, no matter how complicated their conceptions.

Kaitlyn crossed the room and stood next to Brody,

staring out into the dusky front yard. A bare tree stood in contrast to the twilit sky—not dark enough for stars—and the horizon was still glowing red from the sunset, spilling pink light over the snow-laden ground.

"Everything okay?" Kaitlyn asked.

"Fine."

She highly doubted that, but she also didn't want to pry any further into family issues. She had enough of her own right now. Nina was asking Kaitlyn about baby names and if she wanted to be in the delivery room…something she'd never expected. She and Nina had never been terribly close, but this pregnancy seemed to change things between them. Nina seemed to need Kaitlyn in a whole new way, and that softened Kaitlyn, too.

"This is probably terrible timing," Kaitlyn said, "but I can't think of a good time to say this."

"Oh?" He looked down at her warily. "What is it now?"

"I talked to Nina today, told her that you'd told me about her pregnancy." She crossed her arms in a protective reflex. "She and Brian are planning on coming for our fathers' birthday party. Since the news is out in the open."

"We can celebrate all of it." Brody's voice sounded hollow. "Birthdays, a wedding, a baby…"

"I thought I'd give you some fair warning."

"Hmm." Brody was silent for several beats, and he turned his attention back out the window. "It's just as well, I guess."

His reaction surprised her. She'd have thought that Nina coming for a victory lap would have been uncomfortable at the very least, but Brody appeared oddly relaxed.

Kaitlyn swallowed. "Really?"

"It is what it is, Kate." He turned from the window and hobbled toward the chair next to the fireplace. "Besides, I have a bone to pick with Brian."

"Not Nina?" Kaitlyn asked. She wasn't too worried about Nina. She was more worried about her sister doing further damage. But his original shock from the news seemed to have worn off. Brody shot her a wry smile as he lowered himself into the chair.

"Like you said before, I probably should have seen this coming with Nina. Brian, on the other hand—"

He didn't finish the statement, and he didn't need to. He had more relationships to sort out than his cancelled engagement, but her mind went back to that look of steel she'd seen earlier and she eyed him speculatively.

"Are you angry?" she asked.

"Of course." He sighed. "And I know what you're thinking. Brian is perfectly safe with me."

"It had crossed my mind." She was silent for a moment, unsure if she was overstepping by asking anything further, but she decided to risk it. "That ranch hand—"

"Nick." Brody nodded. "My dad is letting him go in the morning. No need to worry about him."

"I was less worried about him than about you," she replied.

"Me?" The look that crossed his face was both surprised and mildly hurt.

"I'm really glad you stepped in," she said, pulling her hair away from her face. "And thank you for that. But, you..." She sucked in a breath, searching for the right words. "You changed."

"How?"

"You looked so much harder, less like you. You went from good old Brody to this steely stranger. I honestly didn't know what you were going to do."

"That's the training." He shrugged apologetically. "Sorry if I scared you."

He had scared her, but at the same time, she knew his instincts had been piqued out of a sense of protectiveness. One thing was certain, that ranch hand would never come near her again. Ironically enough, that was something that hadn't changed a bit—Brody's protective instinct toward her.

"You always did stick up for me. Now you're just... more lethal."

Brody laughed at her dry joke and leaned his head back in the chair. The smile slowly slid from his face, and he turned his dark gaze onto her.

"I will never hurt you," he said softly. "You know that, right?"

She nodded, a lump rising in her throat. "I know."

"That was to protect you, Kate. You're safe with me."

All but her heart. He was so strong and capable, so sad and broken, all at once. He was the kind of man Kaitlyn could love for a lifetime, and if she weren't careful, she would…a lifetime of loving him from afar. That would be hell on earth. Brody leaned forward toward the fire once more.

"You know what I want, more than anything else right now?" he asked.

She shook her head.

"I want to ride Champ at full gallop and just go and go and go…" He heaved a sigh. "You know that feeling? Wind chapping your face, hands cold on the reins, but the sky is just so big and the sun sparkles on the snow… That's how I've always taken care of the things I can't control—on horseback. But I can't ride. I can't even walk without crutches."

"For now," she said quietly.

"I can't fix any of this, Kate." Emotion choked off his voice, and he looked away. After a moment he continued, "But if I could ride…"

It was the cowboy in him, the guy who connected to the land and his horse and the sky. It was the part of him that had put down roots into this very land, the part that had stayed here in spirit no matter how far away he'd roamed. She understood that impulse better than anyone, and she reached out and took his broad, warm hand in hers.

"You'll ride again, Brody," she said firmly. "I promise."

Because from the look in his eyes, if he couldn't ride, they'd most certainly lose him.

Chapter Six

Brody woke early the next morning. The sky was still dark and the house was silent. His parents had already left for chores an hour ago. He'd heard them shuffle about, their low voices filtering through the wall as they tossed back a mug of coffee, pushed their feet into gum boots and headed out. There was something about being back in this familiar house that reset his body to the old alarm clock.

Brody lay there in bed, awake, for what felt like an eternity, but turned out to be a little less than an hour. He didn't want to sleep again. The dreams had been too vivid to properly shake, so he tried to think about something else—anything else, really—and he came up with Kaitlyn's words the night before... Nina and Brian were coming for the party.

He'd brushed it off earlier, because he'd figured having a chance to have it out with Brian would feel cathartic, but this morning he dug a little deeper and wondered what it would be like to see them together.

Nina was notably absent upon his return, so he hadn't been faced with Nina's new life. Instead, he'd been faced with Kaitlyn, and at the moment, he found her more disconcerting. She was no longer the mousy, girlish student. She was now every inch a woman, and he couldn't exactly pinpoint what had changed, but something most definitely had.

Brody swung his legs over the edge of the bed and realized that his wounded leg ached less than it had before. His crutches leaned against the wall next to him, and he reached for them, then stopped short.

"No," he said aloud.

If he wanted to ride, he couldn't be hobbling around on crutches. He needed to be able to walk on his own, and if he didn't push through the pain, it wasn't going to happen.

Brody's grandfather had been in the army, too, and he was the reason Brody had been so enthralled with all things military. Granddad was a lot like Ken Mason—tough and serious—except he wasn't half so stubborn as Brody's father. He could reconsider his position, admit to being wrong. Ken Mason didn't flex. So while Brody and his father butted heads, Granddad told stories about battles and buddies, and gave Brody an escape. Every year on Memorial Day, Granddad stood tall and proud and saluted the flag. Until the year he had his stroke and ended up in a wheelchair, trying to learn how to bring a spoon to his mouth all over again. Brody had been fourteen.

That year, the President of the United States came to the local Memorial Day celebrations. It was close to an election, and the president had made an unplanned stop in their little unknown town. When the president made a short speech thanking the men who gave their all, and the men who served, everyone stood and saluted, including Brody. But then, he noticed Granddad pushing himself forward in his chair.

"Granddad, it's okay," Brody had said, thinking that the old man was confused, but he brushed Brody off and struggled to his feet.

His granddad had wavered there, a tremulous hand raised to his temple in a salute.

The president stopped and said a few words to Granddad on his way back to the bulletproof bus, and Brody saw tears moisten the old man's eyes.

"What did he say?" Brody asked, once the president had gone.

"He thanked me for my service," Granddad replied with a nod. "And he said I didn't need to stand to salute him. I said I sure did. He's my commander in chief."

If Granddad could rise out of that chair to salute, then Brody could stand up on his own two feet and walk to the fence and back. Or the barn. Or the road... It was going to hurt—that was a guarantee—but if he wanted to be more than this injury, he'd have to push past it.

Brody rose to his feet and stood there for a few beats.

"I can do this," he muttered to himself, and an image came to his mind of Kaitlyn's upturned face. For once he'd like to see her expression mirror back something other than concern. He might be wounded, but that didn't make him any less of a man. Once—

just once—he wanted to look down into those chocolate brown eyes and see her respond to him like the man he was.

A good part of him was doing this for her—for that moment when he could stop being her patient and start being... He didn't even know. That was going too far. At the very least he'd like to be a valid threat to her peace of mind, and not because of his relationship to her sister, either.

Getting dressed was easier this morning. As he pulled on his shirt, he stared at the tattered Valentine for several seconds before he scooped it up and tucked it into his pocket. It had been there for the last year, and home or not, he couldn't quite let go of that tradition. Good luck, the guys called it. Maybe it was, because somehow that scrap of paper made him feel stronger.

He hobbled into the kitchen and decided not to stop for food or coffee. He couldn't lose his momentum. He pulled on his fleece-lined jacket and dropped his beaten cowboy hat onto his head, and it felt right.

"To the fence."

The three steps didn't pose as much of a problem as they had earlier, and he realized with a rush of optimism that he was healing. His leg itched now, and while he doubted that he'd ever get away from the ache entirely, he knew it was a good sign.

He'd feel better still when he was slinging bales of hay and saddling up his horse, but he'd take what he could get, and this felt pretty good. Was he really thinking about farm work instead of army training?

He'd have to think about it all more seriously once his body was back into shape.

The morning sunlight filtered across the rolling snow-clad fields. He took a few steps, his gait halting, and then he sucked in a chestful of crisp air and purposely put more weight onto the bad leg.

He suppressed a moan as the pain shot through his thigh, and he stood there for a moment, regaining his sense of balance as his head swam.

"To the fence," he reminded himself firmly.

The fence he'd set as a goal was across the back lawn, separating field from house. The field was covered in a white mantle, some tufts of tough grass sticking up from the snow cover, jutting out in silent rebellion. A swarm of sparrows lifted like a flapping sheet from a copse of bare trees, circled, then came back to settle again on the same limbs.

Across the field and down a gully, he could make out a pickup truck heading into a field, bales of hay loaded into the bed. They'd be filling feeders. As the temperature dropped, the cattle would eat more to maintain their body heat and adjust their metabolism.

Every winter when they were kids, Brian had come to Brody's place for a sleepover. Brian was a town kid, so the idea of ranch chores was exciting to him. They'd ridden in the back of his dad's pickup truck at dawn and helped toss hay out to the cows, and Brian thought it was the best thing ever. Brody smiled at the memory, then pushed it back. That was a long time ago—back when Brian was a trusted friend...

and before Brody had started dreaming of a life away from this place.

But once he did get away, he started longing for this ranch, picturing mornings just like this one...except he'd be the one hauling hay. Like the sparrows that rose up in a swarm only to settle onto the same branches once more. Except now that he was back, he wondered if he could stay.

Was it possible to fit into his life here in Hope again? Maybe it would be different with their father. Dakota seemed pretty convinced that their dad had softened since his injury, and while he'd backed down when it came to firing Nick Sutton, he hadn't turned into a kitten, either.

Brody walked steadily forward, his leg cramping with the effort, but he wouldn't pause. Whether he could make a life here on the ranch or whether he'd go back to the army, he wasn't sure. But the one thing he knew, he wouldn't be spending his life on crutches. Whichever way he went, he'd be doing it on his own two feet.

An engine rumbled in the driveway, and he glanced back to see Kaitlyn's truck come to a stop next to the house. The fence was close, and he turned back toward his goal. His leg ached so badly that it felt like lava was crawling up toward his groin. Three more steps. Two more...okay, maybe another two more...

And then he put out his hand and slapped the wooden rung.

"To the fence," he muttered in victory.

He'd done it. He'd walked to the fence without

crutches, and he leaned against the sturdy rails, breathing heavily.

"Brody?" Kaitlyn's voice rang out in the morning air, and he lifted his head. She was standing beside her truck, hands on her hips. Her glossy hair whipped away from her face in a rising wind, and she raised a hand to her eyes, shading her face against the slant of the sunlight.

Was she ever beautiful.

"Hey!" he called. "Thought I'd come out for a walk."

She said something that didn't carry, but it sounded like a curse and he laughed softly. He must be feeling better, because ticking her off was proving to be a lot of fun. He'd have to find new and creative ways to do more of that. When she was irritated, she looked like she wanted to smack him, and nurses didn't smack patients. At least they weren't supposed to. And more to the point, women didn't slap men they pitied. It was a step in the right direction.

Kaitlyn headed across the grass to meet him.

KAITLYN WAS IMPRESSED by the distance Brody had travelled without his crutches. He stood out there by the fence, cowboy hat pushed back while he leaned his forearms against the top rail, face bathed in early morning sunlight. His breath hung in the cold air.

He looked like the old Brody standing there, and her heart filled with sad longing. How many times had she seen Brody looking just like this? He was strong, handsome, rugged…and unavailable. How many times had she reminded herself of that?

But still—walking around the yard on his own was a risk in itself. He should have waited for her. How on earth had he managed the steps outside the house alone? If he fell right now—a distinct possibility given the ice and snow—he could possibly tear open the newly healed flesh and set himself back weeks in recovery. As scary as that possibility was, it was easier to think of things as a nurse—she felt more in control of her own feelings when she focused on her profession.

"What are you doing out here?" she asked as she reached him.

Brody glanced down at her, amusement sparkling in his gaze. "What does it look like?"

It looked foolhardy. "And your pain on a scale of one to ten?"

Brody looked away again. "I'm not going to tell you."

He was the most stubborn patient she'd come across, and that included an old man who believed that her place was in the kitchen. What was she coming out here for every day if he wasn't going to listen to her or give her the information she needed to do her job? They were paying her for medical care, and that was what she was trying to provide.

"Brody—"

"Can't you stop being my nurse for a few minutes and just be my overly serious Kate again?"

His words stopped her short, and she felt heat rise

in her cheeks. It had been a long time since he'd called her "overly serious." She remembered how he used to needle her when she was trying to study—anything to distract her. She'd put up a token fight, but they both knew he'd win.

"You hated it when I was serious," she said.

"Not true." He cast her a wry smile. "You were a challenge."

A challenge...but he'd been in love with her sister. He might have spent hours sitting around with Kaitlyn, but he'd only been there because he was picking up Nina. And once Nina was ready, she and Brody disappeared into the night, and Kaitlyn had been left at home with her textbooks. She might have had Brody's company and jokes, but her sister had been the one in his arms.

"So what am I supposed to do, if I'm not allowed to be your nurse right now?" she asked.

Brody shrugged. "Just stand there. Look at the cattle. Breathe."

He had a point—she'd been so busy with school and nursing jobs that she'd gotten used to her hectic pace. In some ways it was easier to be busy, because that way she didn't have time to feel sorry for herself. When she dropped into bed at night, she liked to fall asleep right away, because lying there, alone with her thoughts, reminded her of what she was missing.

She saw the tip of the Valentine card poking out of his front pocket and felt a smile come to her lips. He still carried it?

"My Valentine," she said softly.

"Hmm?" He looked down at his pocket and nodded. "Yeah. I kept it."

It was sweet that a simple little gesture had meant that much to him—enough to keep it through his training, his deployment, his mission...

"Why did you keep it?" she asked.

"I don't know." He shook his head. "You struck a cord, I guess. You called me brave."

"It was true." It wasn't the truth she would have liked to say, but she'd made do with that.

"You might need to give me a new one," he said with a short laugh. "I need one that says, 'The scars are hardly noticeable, Valentine.'"

Kaitlyn laughed. "No, I'll stick with brave."

He nodded, his expression sobering. "We all had something that we held on to for good luck. Jeff had his daughter's hair ribbon."

"Jeff is a friend of yours?" she asked.

"Was." Brody cleared his throat. "He died."

There was something in his stance that sank at those words. His gaze turned leaden and he looked away. There was more to Jeff's death than the loss of a buddy—she could feel it.

"In the same explosion that wounded you?" she guessed.

"Yeah."

They were both silent for a few beats as Kaitlyn considered this new information. What had happened out there? What had those men been through?

"I saw it—it was like slow motion. Jeff's boot hit the wire, and I saw it flex and pull. I didn't have time to do anything. If I had, I would have pulled him back, but he was out of reach, and…" He sighed. "I've gone over it a thousand times since. Could I have warned him?"

"Oh, Brody…" Tears misted her eyes and she put a hand on his forearm. "I'm so sorry."

"It wasn't just him. Two other guys died in the same blast—Steve and Raj. The four of us trained together and were posted in the same unit."

She remained silent—she had no answers or platitudes to offer. He'd seen things she couldn't imagine, and she couldn't make any of this better.

"Jeff had three kids. Raj was newly married. Steve didn't have any kids—like me—but he was paying for a nephew to go to a school for gifted children. That boy could do calculus in his head at the age of five, and if Steve weren't paying his way, he'd have fallen through the cracks in public school." He sucked in a deep breath. "If I could have traded places with one of them…"

Did he think no one would care if he'd lived or died? Did he think his presence in this town meant nothing to the rest of them?

"You have people who would have been broken, too, if you hadn't come back."

"Like Nina? I think it would have made things easier for her."

Like Nina? No, Nina was capable of guilt, too, and she would have carried her own burden for the rest of her life. His parents would have been a wreck. Dakota, too.

No one would have thought of Kaitlyn—of that she was positive—but she would have grieved more deeply than anyone imagined. Worrying about Brody, praying for his safety, going through the motions of facing each day without him coming by the house or calling for something or other…it had made her realize how much she'd loved him and how desperately she needed to let go of that.

"Like me." Kaitlyn's voice shook as the words came out, and she blinked back tears that welled up in her eyes. "So don't you say that you don't matter, because if you'd died over there—"

She was saying too much, and she bit back the words. What was she going to do, confess that she'd been in love with him for the two years he'd been dating her sister? It didn't matter. He'd made his choice.

"Hey…" His voice was a low rumble, and he put a finger under her chin and tipped her face up so he could look into her eyes. His gaze moved slowly over her face. "You saying you missed me?"

He arched an eyebrow, and a smile flickered at one side of his mouth. She was saying a whole lot more than that—at least she had been before she'd wisely shut up. Brody ran his thumb along her jaw, the movement slow and deliberate.

She didn't answer him. He was joking around, wasn't he?

And while she wasn't certain a second ago, the moment suddenly deepened, and she caught her breath. His gaze dropped to her lips, dark and hungry, and she'd never felt less in control. She was his nurse, but he was *not* acting like her patient. She could only imagine how much pain he was in right now with his weight on his bad leg, but his gaze didn't waver.

Kaitlyn licked her lips, and Brody leaned closer, his thumb coming to rest on her chin, just under her mouth. He tugged down gently, parting her lips. She longed to just close her eyes and lean into his arms, but she didn't dare. Brody wasn't backing down, either, and just as Brody shifted his weight and closed the gap between them, the heat of his body settling against hers, the growl of an engine came up the back road and a horn tooted cheerfully. Brody pulled back, and Kaitlyn's knees nearly buckled right there. Given another moment uninterrupted, would he have kissed her?

Would she have let him?

She closed her eyes and swallowed hard. He was toying with her—at least it felt that way. If he knew how she really felt about him, he wouldn't play so freely, but he probably felt safe in the fact that he was the one in control and he could pull away anytime he liked. She was "overly serious Kate," and maybe he thought he was doing her a favor, getting her to lighten up. But her heart didn't play these games so smoothly, and she didn't have time to examine her own feelings right now. She pasted a smile on her face as the old beat-up ranch truck came up over a hill and Dakota waved from the driver's seat.

Frankly, she was grateful for Dakota's timing. Kissing her patient wasn't professional, but more than that... While she'd dreamed of Brody seeing her as more than Nina's little sister, seeing the woman in her the way she saw the man in him, it wasn't right. She knew that look—the very look he'd given her sister before he'd driven off for the bus station that last time, heading for boot camp, her small gift of a Valentine's Day card tucked in the side pocket of his duffle bag.

Kaitlyn would never be a man's consolation prize—not even Brody Mason's.

Chapter Seven

When they got back inside the house, Kaitlyn busied herself with Brody's medication charts—double-checking her work—but her mind kept wandering. That moment by the fence had her feeling rather breathless still.

Brody was in the other room, which was what she needed right now—a physical distance between herself and the wounded cowboy, because the sparks hadn't been one-sided this time...

She poured herself some coffee into the first cup she grabbed from the cupboard. It was a joke mug that read *Déjà Moo: when you've seen this BS before.* She smiled wryly. The mug might prove prophetic. She'd seen friends pine over cowboys who never gave them a second look, only to have their hearts broken when a weak moment and a beer too many fanned sparks that had no hope of igniting without the alcohol. Pining was pathetic, and Kaitlyn had determined not to be that kind of woman, yet here she was.

And he'd kept the Valentine...carried it with him. What did that mean? Was it just a soldier thing—a good luck charm that had carried him through tough times? Because while he'd carried that card with him—unknown to her—he'd never hinted at feeling more than friendship for her in their emails. It was only today, standing by the fence, that he'd seemed to feel anything stronger.

He was going to kiss me...

Or was he? If Dakota hadn't driven up when she had, he might still have come to his senses and pulled back. She was his nurse, after all, and he wasn't an idiot. Maybe—and this thought came with a stab— he'd only contemplated the idea because of her resemblance to her sister. And she didn't look that much like her sister, so the momentary lapse would have stayed very momentary.

What Brody needed was to get over Nina, and distracting himself with her—the only woman he'd had contact with for the last couple of weeks whom she wasn't related to—wasn't the answer. Kaitlyn knew this, so why was it so difficult for her?

"Kate."

She turned to see Brody standing in the doorway to the kitchen. He leaned one shoulder against the wall and his dark eyes drilled into her.

"Do you want a coffee?" She raised her cup.

"No, thanks." He took a deep breath, then cleared his throat. "Look, out there—"

"Don't mention it. Nothing happened." She gave him a tight smile and brought her coffee to the kitchen table. She'd go through his prescriptions and see which needed refills. That should keep her grounded.

"Things are different now," he said quietly.

"That's an understatement." She couldn't help the sarcasm that leaked into her tone.

"I mean between you and me."

"The only difference I can see," she said, "is that my sister isn't here."

Brody didn't answer, but he did cross the room and sink into a kitchen chair opposite her. How on earth was she going to keep working as Brody's nurse if they couldn't get some of this straightened out? She had feelings for him, but she also had several years of experience in pushing them down, so she was relatively confident she could continue with that...as long as he continued treating her like a buddy. That had been their arrangement—and what almost happened by the fence couldn't happen again.

"See, you keep saying that I've changed," Kaitlyn went on. "But I haven't. I was right under your nose looking exactly like this—"

"You wore more ponytails back then," he interrupted.

"As if that's the defining difference." She shook her head. "Hair back or down, I'm pretty much the same, Brody. The only thing that's changed is that Nina isn't around. If she were, trust me, you'd still see me as that little sister in a ponytail."

"Are you saying that having Nina in the city hasn't changed things for you?" he demanded.

Kaitlyn frowned and put her pen down with a click. "I'm more visible. That's about it."

Brody sighed and leaned back. "I get it. I completely overstepped out there, and I'm sorry."

It wasn't only him. She could have stepped back at any point, but she hadn't. She'd wanted to simply let herself go in the moment and regret it later. She could tell herself otherwise all she wanted, but that was the truth. She knew every single reason not to kiss Brody, and she'd been willing to let all of them go.

"It's only because you miss Nina," she said with more confidence than she felt.

"No, it isn't." His voice was low, and when she looked up, his dark gaze was fixed on her. "For once, that had nothing to do with your sister."

Kaitlyn pulled in a shaky breath. Could she believe that? Brody obviously did, but he wouldn't be the first man to deceive himself.

"Are you sure about that?" she asked with a small smile. "I know the impact my sister has on men, so—"

"It wears off."

Kaitlyn frowned. "I thought you were crazy about her."

Brody sighed. "I'm moving on. What would you have me do, Kate?"

Fair enough. What did she expect him to do, exactly? Pine forever to prove his loyalty to a woman who didn't want him?

"I let myself get carried away earlier," he said. "And maybe you're right—maybe you're just as gorgeous as you always were, and I just never saw it. But for whatever reason, I've been noticing lately. You're not the kid sister anymore."

"Thank you." Heat rose in her cheeks. "It's nice to be noticed. But I'm your nurse, Brody. I'm the one who takes care of your injury, and blurring those lines makes things really complicated. Trust me on that."

"I know." He didn't elaborate, and she found herself wondering if he was imagining the same thing she was—namely, that he'd give her a few toe-curling kisses and then realize that she comforted him when he needed it but that was all it was, and they'd be awkward together ever after.

"I know you'll move on…probably a few times… and it's Nina's loss." Kaitlyn swallowed hard. "But I'm not available for that, Brody. I'm here to be your nurse. We need to keep those boundaries solid."

"Not a friend?" he asked quietly.

"And a friend… Of course, we're friends. But when I'm taking out your stitches and you're swearing at me for making you stretch in ways that hurt like crazy, you're going to be glad that I'm your nurse and nothing more."

"I got carried away, that's all. I don't think I'll be sticking around town anyway once I'm healed, so it's just as well. It won't happen again."

She stared at him for a moment, and the blood rushed to her head so that all she could hear was a ringing in her ears. Dakota had mentioned the same thing, but hearing it from him brought the possibility down with the pressure of a branding iron. She shouldn't be surprised. This was exactly why she needed to keep her professional reserve. She swallowed, looked away and then said, "Speaking of stitches, we should take those out today."

Kaitlyn was used to this feeling—being in love with a man she'd never have. She could shoulder this for the both of them. Brody was shouldering horrific memories of his own, and that was part of his sacrifice for his country. The least she could do was protect him from any further indignity.

And she needed to protect herself, too, because while Brody had experienced some passing attraction, she was trying to get over feelings that went much deeper. They were both nursing broken hearts...and only one of them could admit to it.

WHEN KAITLYN LEFT, leaving him to rest, Brody stood at the kitchen sink for a long time. He was tired and his leg ached, but he was upright, and that was what mattered. If army training taught him anything, it was *no pain, no gain*.

He didn't blame Kaitlyn. Look at him—wounded, limping and certainly not the man she remembered from a year ago... He couldn't blame her if she hadn't felt the same attraction that he had. He'd been looking into the warm and sensitive eyes of a woman who'd only grown more beautiful. And she knew exactly what kind of man she deserved.

Not him.

That stung, but it didn't surprise him. He'd come home with nightmares, pain meds and a track record of not being enough for his buddies or for his fiancée. And while he couldn't quite understand why he hadn't been able to see exactly how alluring Kaitlyn was before he left, he could only suppose it was because he was loyal.

Nina hadn't been perfect, and neither was Brody, but he was the kind of guy who stayed true to the woman he was with. He didn't stray. He didn't play the field. And he certainly wasn't the kind of guy who made a move on his nurse.

He grimaced. What had he been thinking? Kaitlyn had put him in his place pretty firmly, and he'd been telling God's honest truth when he promised it wouldn't happen again. He was determined that it wouldn't. While she'd seemed equally drawn to him out there by the fence, once she'd been able to think it through, she'd changed her mind. While he liked a challenge, he didn't like being the guy that a woman *knew* was terrible for her, even if he could tempt her to ignore her gut a few times. He wasn't a snake with an apple. He was a man who wanted the real thing—love, home, family.

His thoughts were interrupted by the sound of his father's boots on the steps outside. Ken came in with a blast of cold air and a swirl of snowflakes that melted on the linoleum floor. He shook the snow off his hat and hung it up, running a gnarled hand through his silvered hair.

Brody and his father didn't have a talkative relationship, and Brody gave his father a silent nod. Ken slowly unzipped his jacket, then cleared his throat.

"I fired Nick Sutton," he said.

Brody nodded. "Good."

"You might have been right about him." Ken's expression betrayed how difficult those words were for him, and Brody eyed his father in surprise.

"Really?"

"He spat on my boot and cursed me to my face."

"So no reference?" Brody asked wryly.

Ken let out a grunt of a laugh. "Guess not."

Brody turned toward the sitting room. He'd have to savor this one—this kind of victory was a rarity around here.

"When you were little I wouldn't let you swim in the deep part of the creek," his father said, his voice like gravel. The words—and the sentiment—came as a surprise. Weren't they supposed to be talking about firing someone?

Brody frowned, turned back. "Yeah. House rules." What was his father getting at?

"And I taught you to never surprise a cow from behind." His father nodded slowly. "And never, ever to take a dare."

Brody stayed silent, watching his father uncertainly. The man's face was creased by weather and time, and his blue eyes looked watery in this midmorning light. He rubbed his calloused hands together.

"It wasn't that I didn't trust you, or that I didn't think you could handle yourself," his father said. "But you were my child. And as a father, I had to protect you." Ken paused, shoved his hands into his front pockets. "That's why I didn't want you to join the army. It wasn't that I didn't think you could handle yourself. I knew you could. I just wanted to make sure you stayed safe."

"I was helping keep America safe," Brody said.

Ken nodded. "And I was supposed to be proud."

The words hit Brody in the chest. *Supposed to be proud.* His father had gone quiet when Brody enlisted in the army, and while aunts and uncles told him that they were so proud of him, his father had never said a word. That silence had been deafening.

"Sorry to disappoint," Brody said bitterly.

"Do you know how it would feel to be given a flag and a few condolences?" Ken asked. "As a parent, do you know how that would feel?"

Brody shook his head. "I came back alive, Dad."

"But your buddies didn't."

As if Brody needed a reminder of that, and he couldn't help the anger that simmered inside of him. His father slowly looked up and met Brody's gaze.

"I couldn't bury you." Ken's voice shook and he pressed his lips together. It wasn't enough to stop his chin from trembling. Brody had never seen his father cry, and his throat grew tight.

"Dad—" Brody started.

"No, I have to say this," his father said, sucking in a deep breath. "I get that a young man needs to follow his own dreams. I was young once, too. But I'm asking you as your father to stay down...tap out. Run this place with me. But please, don't go back there. If I had to bury you, I don't think I'd survive it."

That was the thing his father didn't understand—

Brody wasn't living his life to make other people comfortable. He had to find somewhere he could contribute, somewhere these memories could fit back in and make sense, because they sure didn't make any sense here on the ranch.

"Tap out?" Brody asked incredulously.

"Bad choice of words." His father winced. "Stay home. I'd ask you not to break your mother's heart, but that wouldn't be honest. Don't break mine."

Tears misted Brody's eyes and he looked away. His father had never spoken to him this directly before, but he was asking for too much.

"Dad, I'm not the same," he said quietly.

"That's okay." His father swallowed hard. "You don't have to be."

And for his father, maybe he didn't. But Brody was the one carrying the burden. He couldn't package up Afghanistan and put it on a shelf. This wasn't a summer of travel after high school. Because if that horror didn't have meaning, then it would crush him.

"I saw stuff, Dad." Brody hadn't spoken of this before—not to a civilian. "When villages have no government to hold them together, the worst people start doing the things that society would have stopped. And as a soldier, you have to choose what you're going to stop and what you're going to look away from. You can't stop it all. And there were too many atrocities I couldn't stop, Dad."

"It wasn't your fault," his father said.

"But I had to choose who I helped and who I

didn't," Brody went on. "I remember their faces. The kids, the women, a teenage boy—"

His voice was choked off. It was just as well. He couldn't burden his old man with this stuff. Civilians didn't know how to cope with this. Neither did soldiers most of the time. That's why they all had the nightmares.

"Even when I didn't have a choice, I feel guilt as if I did—because I might have been able to choose differently, make a better call."

"You made a good call with Nick," his father said.

The situation with Nick was so much smaller than the kind of pain he was carrying around.

"But that wasn't life-or-death," Brody said bitterly. "That was just a creep who needed to move on."

His father shrugged sadly. "You'd never have to see that again if you stayed home."

Brody sighed. If only it were just a matter of choosing a place to live. It was more than that—it was choosing a place where he could go on living.

"I don't know what to say," Brody said at last. He had no answers, no solutions. He had no absolution for the friends who had died, the innocent civilians who had looked to him to intervene...

"It's okay," his father said. "I've got a fence to mend. I just wanted to say my bit. Give it some thought."

Why did coming home have to be so complicated? He had sins to atone for, and he couldn't atone by mending fences and wrangling cattle. And he bloody well didn't deserve the peace he longed for.

Chapter Eight

The next morning, Brody sat in front of the TV watching the news channel. He'd never been a huge news watcher in the past, having the pessimistic view that anything real wouldn't make it onto the news networks anyway, but since coming back, he found himself hypervigilant. The news might be exaggerated and biased, but it was a glimpse into the outside world, that vast space just past the confines of Hope.

An army correspondent came on the screen, one finger pressed into her ear, and a microphone held close to her mouth. Overhead the whistle of a missile made her hunch down, and then the sky in the distance glowed red with an explosion. Brody's pulse hammered in his neck and he flicked off the TV. It was one thing to be in a battle zone when you had orders to follow and you could do something. It was altogether different to watch from the easy chair in the living room, his morning coffee getting cold beside him.

Nothing was the same anymore, and he knew that to think all this through he needed to ride and there was no way he was going to get Kaitlyn's support in that so early.

Kaitlyn. What was it about her that kept his mind coming back to her? He was a glutton for punishment—rejected by one sister and falling for the other. Maybe those words were too strong—he was most certainly *not* falling for his pretty nurse. She was just that perfect mixture of strength and innocence that made him hope for some sort of comfort.

It wasn't just their shared history, either, because she was no longer the college student in a ponytail. She was now his nurse…and currently, she was running a few errands while he was supposed to be resting.

Resting! He wasn't an old man or an invalid, but Kaitlyn insisted that he allow his body time to heal. Rest wasn't helping—not mentally, at least. The last thing he needed was more uninterrupted time with his own thoughts.

"I'm spending too much time inside," he muttered, pushing himself up from the easy chair. The news channel wasn't helping matters, and neither were his family's hopes that he'd stay in Hope. He needed to ride. Wasn't that what he'd been saying all along? Besides, Kaitlyn wasn't here to talk him out of it, so now was the time to make it happen.

His leg ached, but not as badly as before, and he tested his range of motion cautiously. His muscles didn't have the same flexibility he used to have, and he could feel the fresh scars tug as he stretched his leg out, then pulled his knee as high as he was able. That hurt.

Brody limped over to the hook where his hat hung and dropped it onto his head. If he waited for the pain to stop, he'd be sitting by the fire for the rest of his life, and that wasn't an option. An image of Kaitlyn's angry face rose in his mind, and he grimaced. She'd be furious if she arrived to find him missing, so he'd do the considerate thing. He scribbled a note on a scrap of paper, left it on the kitchen table and pulled open the door.

Ten minutes later, Brody was limping down the gravel drive that led to the barn. The cold air stung his face, and his breath came out in a cloud. The fields glistened like crushed diamonds, and the barn, freshly painted red, brought with it all those feelings of home. In moments like this, he wished he *could* stay. Brody paused to catch his breath and leaned forward, putting a hand on his thigh. His leg ached from the exertion, and he found himself idly longing for the warmth of the fire to soak away a bit of the pain. The mental image of an old man by the hearth kept him moving in the right direction.

Never before had this road seemed so arduous or long, but he wasn't about to give up. He needed this more than anyone seemed to realize. Before he'd left for the army, Brody had known who he was. He was the son of a grisly rancher, and he was determined to make a career for himself as far from home as possible. But it turned out that no matter how far you roamed, home sat inside of you and it seemed all the more achingly beautiful for how far you'd gone. He was home—right back to the place he'd dreamed of and longed for when he was dodging bullets—and he'd never felt further away.

Brody straightened and started his limping gait once more. He needed to ride, and that was his single-minded mission of the day. He'd ride Champ, or he'd pass out in the attempt.

KAITLYN LOOKED DOWN at the note in the center of the kitchen table:

Kate, I've gone riding. Care to join me?

This wasn't exactly a surprise. He'd been push-ing himself to the limit since he'd returned, and she knew he longed to be on horseback again. Her heart dropped, though, because of what this meant. Brody wasn't going to stay in Hope. He had nothing left here—nothing that mattered to him, at least. He wasn't aiming to ranch and ride and rope. He was pushing this hard to get out for good.

And it was her job to help him recover, except the pace he'd set for himself was inhuman. He couldn't keep this up without doing some major damage to his already-wounded body. It was selfish and horrible, but she did hope that regaining full mobility took a little longer. She didn't want him to suffer. She just wanted him to stay.

Kaitlyn didn't bother taking off her coat or gloves, and she headed back out the door and down the steps. She'd take her truck to the barn—Heaven knew what shape he'd be in by the time she got to him, and she highly doubted he'd be in any condition to walk up-hill to the house.

She hopped into the truck and turned the key, muttering to herself about the stupidity of stubborn men. Griping was easier than crying right now. She could deal with grumpy old men or forgetful old ladies who thought she was their dead husbands' mistress... None of that was personal. Brody was worse, because he insisted on relating to her as Kate, not as his professional medical care provider, tugging her closer and closer, all with the intention of walking away. But while he was here, he needed her for more than just nursing care—he needed her friendship, her emotional support. There was nothing simple about this position. Brody took a job and made it achingly personal.

She turned onto the road that led to the barn and followed it, steering around the potholes. When she parked, she hopped out of the truck and headed toward the open corral door.

"Brody?"

As she came around the side of the barn, she saw Brody standing on the block used for teaching kids how to mount. In Brody's condition, he would never get onto Champ's back by simply swinging up, and she silently wished he hadn't thought of the block. It would be a whole lot easier to argue him down if he weren't already in the saddle.

"Hey," Brody said, glancing back. "I see you got my note."

"I did." Her tone was dry and she shook her head. "What do you think you're doing?"

"Disobeying orders." He shot her a teasing grin. "You aren't half as scary as an army general, you know."

She rolled her eyes. "I'm not trying to be scary. I'm trying to point out reason. That's going to hurt a lot, you know."

"It already does," he retorted. "Are you going to help me or let me tear something?"

Help him? Was he serious? What he needed was another week of rest, and then several weeks of physiotherapy. This was not good for him.

"If you allow your body to heal more before you start riding again, you can do this without the pain." She'd try logic. Maybe he'd respond to that.

"It's going to hurt when I start riding again, regardless," he shot back.

"It'll hurt significantly less if you've healed!" Why was he being so bullheaded? Was he in that much of a hurry to get away?

Brody turned and caught her eye with his dark magnetic gaze, and the memory of lips hovering over hers came back so strongly that her cheeks grew warm. She broke eye contact and looked away.

He said quietly, "I'm going to give this a try with or without your help. It'll hurt—I know that—but I have a theory that it'll hurt less if you give me a hand."

That wasn't even fair. She sighed and opened the gate in the side of the paddock and came around to where Champ stood, breathing out great billows of steam. She guided Champ closer to the block—taking a quick tug on the straps to make sure they were tight—then angled around Champ's rippling shoulder.

"You sure about this?" she asked.

He shot her a grin. "Nope, but I'm doing it anyway."

Brody put his foot in the stirrup, then grimaced as he tried to swing his injured leg up, but it wouldn't go high enough. That was what physiotherapy would be for—and that wouldn't start until she'd deemed him healed enough for the stretching.

Or would he leave before he could ride? It was a possibility that occurred to her only now. His leg came back down to the block and he let out a huff of breath. Champ looked back at Brody, liquid eyes pinned questioningly to his master. She could see how he would have to do this...was she really going to suggest a way to make this insanity possible?

"You'll have to put your bad leg in the stirrup," Kaitlyn said. "Do you think you could hold your weight for that long?"

Brody shrugged. "Let's find out."

"I don't like this," she said, for the record.

"Right now, you aren't my nurse," he said, one side of his mouth turning up in a smile.

"I most certainly am!" she retorted.

"We'll have to agree to disagree on that one," he said, coming down from the mounting block and walking Champ around so he could mount from the other side.

Kaitlyn stood next to Champ's shoulder and this time, when he put his boot into the stirrup, she put a supporting hand on his calf to help hold him steady as he swung the other leg over. The blood drained from his face with the effort, but he was mounted, and he breathed heavily for a moment before he glanced down and caught her eye.

"I'm going to do this every day until it doesn't hurt anymore."

Brody make a clicking sound with his mouth, and he and Champ started out at a walk. Even at that slow pace, the movement would be excruciating for Brody, and she wished he would listen to her. But then, he wouldn't be Brody Mason, would he? He didn't leave the corral, and as he rode slowly around the perimeter, she could tell that Champ was doing his best to be gentle.

He was going to do this every day until it stopped hurting—much like she was doing right now by forcing herself to put a professional smile on her face and pretend that she felt nothing more than friendly concern or medical caution.

Perhaps they weren't so different after all, because she had the same mantra—you got out by going through. Except, the pain that Brody was pushing himself through was different than hers. His would heal, and over time he'd lose most of his limp and the scars would cover that tender place where the pain had been the worst. He'd move on. He'd find another woman to love, and Kaitlyn would be nothing but a memory—the sister of the woman he almost married, who acted as his nurse for a few weeks.

But what about her? Would she be able to move

on without an emotional hitch? She'd hoped that this process would be her healing, too, but now she wasn't so sure. If Brody had been the same laughing goof he was when he left, it might have been possible, but he wasn't. He'd deepened and broadened, and if it were possible, she was risking falling for him in a much more dangerous way.

Chapter Nine

The next few days, Kaitlyn watched as Brody made good on his promise to ride daily. Every afternoon, he limped to the corral and he rode Champ. The third day, he took the horse out of the corral and into the field and Kaitlyn stood by the fence watching them. There was something about Brody on horseback—she could almost feel his burdens lifting in the whistle of the winter wind. Brody was much like Dakota in the skill he used handling horses, and watching him ride reminded her that this instinct went bone deep in the Masons. He might have changed over the last year, experienced things that would haunt him for the rest of his life, but if he was going to heal on the inside, he needed to find a piece of his old self again.

On the fourth morning after a longer ride than usual, Kaitlyn leaned against the gate of Champ's stall as Brody brushed him down. The morning was bright and the sunlight that flooded through the window felt warm against her legs. Outside it was cold, but inside the barn was cozy and the hay-scented air tickled her nose.

Brody straightened and put a hand on his thigh with a wince. He'd be in pain, there was no doubt about it, but he was happier with his horse.

"What's on your mind?" he asked without looking at her.

She smiled wanly. "How do you do that?"

He glanced over. "You're tense. It shows."

She sighed. "You're recovering nicely."

"Thanks." He shot her a grin. "Is that a problem?"

He was teasing, but she was serious. "You don't need me full-time anymore."

"Okay." He eyed her uncertainly, the rhythmic strokes with the grooming brush slowing to a stop. "Do you have another job you want to take?"

"No."

Watching him ride this last week, she'd desperately wished he could find that missing piece of himself in their time together...but she wasn't enough. She never had been.

"You just want to be paid less?" He raised an eyebrow.

"No." She swallowed hard and ran a hand through her hair. "It's not about the money, Brody. This is... We're..." How on earth was she supposed to explain this? What was she supposed to do, tell him that she'd had a crush on him for years, and that being this close to him was making it hard to draw those lines? A woman didn't just bare her heart like that.

"Is it the day I almost kissed you?" His voice was low, and heat rose in her face at the memory of that hungry look in his eye.

"Sort of," she agreed. "I'm your nurse, but we also have some history. It complicates things. For us, at least."

"And if I give you my word of honor to keep my lips to myself?" There was a spark of humor in his eye, and she smiled wanly. It wasn't only that moment by the fence.

"You almost kissing me—it wasn't your fault alone," she admitted quietly. "I'm your nurse. It's my job to keep it professional, and…"

And she was having trouble doing that. She wouldn't be able to turn him away if he were to try and kiss her again…even now. And she needed to be the stronger of them. He needed her to be, but she was playing with fire and she knew it.

"You're my ex-fiancée's sister, and this is uncomfortable for you," he concluded.

"Yes." The word came out in a rush of relief. That covered it quite nicely. It went deeper, but that was the essence.

"I get it." There was a heaviness in his tone, but he turned back to the brushing. Champ's flank shivered with pleasure at the strokes. The joking was gone from his voice, and she wondered what he was thinking.

"I'm sorry," she added. "I think it's for the best. You need other people around you. Not just me."

"I've been clingy, have I?" he asked, glancing toward her again.

He'd been the opposite of clingy, actually. He'd been irritatingly independent, but that hadn't made this any easier on her emotionally. She was supposed to be getting over her feelings, paying her penance for having been part of the lie, not getting more attached.

"It's just hard for me," she said finally, her voice catching. "This is better. Trust me. I'll still be your nurse. Just not round-the-clock."

Her cell phone rang, echoing shrilly in the closed space, and her focus was momentarily shaken. Kaitlyn glanced down at the number.

"It's Mackenzie Granger," she said.

"Answer it." Brody put his muscle into the grooming once more, his expression impenetrable. She paused, watching him as he worked. The phone rang again, and she picked up the call.

"Hi, Mack," she said, trying to sound normal.

"Hi, Kaitlyn. How are you doing?"

"Not too bad." A lie, but it was unavoidable. "What can I do for you?"

"Am I on speaker?" Mack asked.

"No." Kaitlyn chuckled. "What's going on?"

"You know how much I love my in-laws, right? Well, they're insane. I mean, completely nuts. I love them dearly, but... Okay, so Chet's aunt Bethany told me in all seriousness that newborns shouldn't be touched too much, *lest they get used to it.* As if we should condition them not to expect affection. They're in the world now, and their emotional needs are their responsibility." Her tone made the eye roll evident. "Then his aunt Maureen told me that the more dirt the better—on premature babies! Their immune systems aren't even fully formed yet. His aunt Felicity says that brandy—brandy!—is a great way to get your twins to sleep at the same time. Just booze them up! I'm exhausted, but that's just crazy. Can you imagine what alcohol would do to a developing brain? I mean, it might explain Cousin Craig, but..."

Kaitlyn laughed. "Wow. Well, I guess you're up for all that mom advice now."

"Here's the problem." Mack's tone softened. "I have a doctor's appointment, and bringing two newborns is going to be hard. I'm still in a lot of pain since the C-section. I was wondering if you'd mind babysitting for a couple of hours. I need someone... normal."

"So the honeymoon has worn off with the Grangers, has it?" Kaitlyn chuckled.

"Like I said, I love them dearly..." There was a wince in her voice.

"I'm joking," Kaitlyn said. "What time is your appointment?"

"Two this afternoon."

This might be the perfect chance to pull away a little bit, get some distance. It would be a welcome distraction, that was for sure.

"I think I could manage that. I also solemnly promise not to rub your babies in dirt or let them cry."

There was a smile in Mackenzie's tone. "Thank you, Kaitlyn. I really appreciate this." She paused. "Oh, and if Brody's around, could you give him a message? Chet wanted his advice on a horse."

That was good for Brody, too—to be needed, to be invited. She covered the mouthpiece.

"Chet needs your advice on a horse," she said.

"Sure." Brody gave one last stroke with the curry-comb and put it on the top of the fence rail.

"Message delivered," Kaitlyn said. "I'll see you later."

When Kaitlyn hung up, Brody was looking at her with one eyebrow arched.

"What's going on, exactly?"

"Something about a horse. I'm sure Chet will fill you in." She crossed her arms over her chest. "And I'm babysitting this afternoon, so I'll be out of your hair for a bit."

She sounded more confident than she felt. This was the right thing to do. Brody didn't need her as a constant companion, and they both needed to live their own lives. Brody's grit had paid off after all, and he was recovering more quickly than anyone hoped possible. He needed less of her, and she needed less of him, even if her desires weren't in sync with what was good for her.

This is a good thing, she reminded herself.

But it was a good thing that ached a little too much like a goodbye.

WHEN BRODY ARRIVED at the Granger ranch, his leg was tight and aching. Kaitlyn's words were still running through his mind. She wanted space—for both of them. It made sense, but he couldn't help but feel like he'd been swatted away. It was his own fault. He was letting himself cross lines with Kaitlyn, and he knew better. And she was right.

"Hey, Brody!" Chet's truck rumbled up, and the tall cowboy cranked down the driver's side window. "Thanks for coming by!"

"No problem." Brody slammed shut his own truck door, stretching his leg out tenderly.

"I've got to check out a situation with some ranch hands. I'll be back in about ten minutes," Chet said. "Just make yourself comfortable in the house, and I'll swing back to pick you up."

"Sure." What else could he say? Except that his nurse was in that house—the very woman trying to get some space from him. Ten minutes to a rancher could be two hours or all day. Brody knew that well enough, and he gave what he hoped was a casual wave as Chet cranked the window back up and rumbled on down the bumpy road.

Brody stood for a moment in the winter chill, then he looked toward the house. He heaved a sigh, and limped in that direction.

When he knocked, Mackenzie Granger opened the door, and she stepped back to usher him in.

"Brody!" She gave him a quick hug. "You look great! How are you doing?"

"Not bad." He smiled. "Congratulations on the babies."

"Thanks." Mackenzie glanced at her watch. "I wish I could stick around to catch up, Brody, but I've got an appointment. Chet will be glad you're here."

"Yeah, I saw him outside. He'll be back in a few minutes."

Kaitlyn stood with both babies in her arms, and

she cast Brody an unreadable look. He gave her a tentative smile.

The Granger ranch house was clean, but cluttered with baby paraphernalia. Two bassinets sat next to a playpen, which had a few boxed toys inside it, as well as a stack of folded blue blankets and a few other gizmos that Brody didn't readily recognize.

"We'll be fine," Kaitlyn said to Mackenzie with a reassuring smile, and Mackenzie bent down to kiss both babies once more.

"I haven't left them yet... This is harder than I thought."

"Call any time you want to check up on them," Kaitlyn said.

"Thanks." Mackenzie hitched her purse on her shoulder. "Two hours. I promise. Maybe less."

As the door shut, Kaitlyn turned toward Brody, a baby in each arm. They were smaller than they seemed they should be—two squished little faces and four tiny fists. They both wore white sleepers, and tiny caps, and there was something softer about Kate with the babies in her arms.

"Hey, before you ask," Brody said, "I'm here to see that horse Chet wants advice about, and he asked me to wait here for a few minutes while he takes care of something."

"I know you aren't following me around," she said, giving him the slightest of smiles. "But you might as well get comfortable. Who knows how long Chet will be."

Brody chose a chair by the window, the playpen

next to him. He eased down, his leg twinging with pain. He rubbed a hand down his thigh.

"Mackenzie's different," Brody said, glancing out the window to where she was starting the truck. In some ways, she was the same old Mack, but she was softer now, carrying some baby weight, but also altered. It was like she'd come back from a battle of her own.

"Motherhood does that." Kaitlyn smiled down at the babies. "Which one do you want?"

"Which what?"

In answer, Kaitlyn placed an infant into his hands and he reached out with fingers splayed as if he were catching a grenade. The tiny rump didn't even fill his palm. He cradled the egg-delicate head with his other hand and stared in panicked surprise into the sleeping face. The baby squirmed and he pulled it close to his chest like a football.

"I think that's Jackson. And I've got Jayden. Aren't they sweet?" Kaitlyn smiled at the infant in her arms and rocked from side to side.

"I don't know what to do with babies," he said, panic rising inside of him. He certainly hadn't signed on for babysitting.

"Don't rub him in dirt, and you should be fine." She shot him a teasing grin. "Cute, aren't they?"

"Cute," he agreed. Actually, they looked wrinkled and stick legged, like little old men with serious expressions, but he was relatively certain that observation wouldn't be appreciated right now.

Brody took a minute to adjust the baby and he

grabbed a blanket from the pile in the playpen next to him. When he got Baby Jackson settled into a nest of blanket in the crook of one arm, he paused to look at him. Jeff had three kids, and the first—a boy—had been born while he was deployed. He'd returned to the States to meet his six-month-old son for the first time. It hadn't been an ideal meeting, and every time he tried to pick up his son, the baby would howl. It took a few weeks for the baby to accept him. What Jeff wouldn't have given to be able to hold his boy at this stage...

He looked up to find Kaitlyn watching him.

"I'd feel better if I was chopping wood or something while I waited," he said with a wry smile. "That would feel more useful."

Kaitlyn rolled her eyes at him, then sank into a rocking chair opposite him. "Sometimes, the most useful thing you can do is just sit there."

"And heal?" he asked ruefully.

Providing a steady heartbeat to a tiny little guy gave him something, too. When he joined the army, he'd pretty much put his own body on the line for America. Ironically, his own flesh and blood seemed to be the most useful thing he could offer, even now. Sitting in a living room with a baby in his arms didn't tamp out the army instinct, though. His right hand stayed free to grab a gun that was no longer at his side—something he hadn't been able to quell since his return.

"See?" she said.

He glanced up to see Kaitlyn looking at him with

a tender expression on her face. She must have noticed a change in him, and truthfully, the tension had seeped from his shoulders and he didn't feel so antsy anymore.

"Yeah, okay..." he said.

Jeff had been luckier than he—he'd had a family. He'd left them too soon, but he'd known what it was like to hold his children in his lap, to vow to love a woman till death parted them. Brody had always assumed he'd get married and have kids one day, but maybe he'd changed too much to have a family of his own. He wasn't the laughing cowboy anymore. He was broken.

Cowboys and soldiers were active men—fighting and wrangling, guarding and providing. They got out there and got 'er done. They were used to solitude and male comradery, and they bloody well didn't go around asking for affection. Sex? Maybe. Brody wasn't the type to find a one-night stand, though. Affection was something deeper than simple sexual release—something he couldn't ask for.

"You know what?" Kaitlyn looked at her watch. "The babies will probably be hungry soon."

She levered herself up from the rocking chair and came to Brody's side. "Take Jayden, too. I'm going to start warming bottles."

Without waiting for a reply, she slipped the second baby into his other arm and he froze. They were both so small, and that instinct to keep his gun hand free was almost overwhelming.

"I need a hand free," he said.

"The minute you can't scratch, your nose will itch," Kaitlyn said.

That wasn't it, but now that she mentioned it...

"Actually—my forehead."

She ran a cool hand over his forehead, and the soft scent of her perfume lingered close. Her touch was silky soft and if he'd had a free hand, he'd have caught that slender wrist and tugged her closer still. Forget the phantom gun. He wasn't feeling all fired up like a teenager. It was something different, something that sank down deeper. It was the lonesome part of him—the side that knew no one else understood but still didn't want to be left alone.

"Better?" she asked.

She had no idea what her touch did to him. An image of exactly what he wanted rose in his mind, but he forced it back.

"Yeah, thanks."

She turned toward the kitchen and Brody watched her walk away. Kaitlyn was a beautiful woman, and he realized in this moment, with infants in his arms, that his longing for her hadn't been the most obvious kind between a man and woman. He hadn't wanted to pull her into his lap and make her breathless...he'd wanted something more elemental.

This was why men chopped wood and wrangled cattle. It gave vent to those deeper feelings with some dignity and hard work. Because when she'd touched his face, he'd longed for a connection much more vulnerable than racing pulses...he'd wanted a hug.

As if on cue, Chet's ranch trunk growled up the

drive and came to a stop outside the window. He was off the hook—Brody breathed a sigh of relief. Time to do what he knew how to do—be a cowboy.

Chapter Ten

Gray clouds scudded across the pale sky as Kaitlyn put her foot into the stirrup and swung into Mary Kay's saddle. She'd been doing her best to keep her distance, watching Brody ride from the fence and keeping her visits short. It wasn't as easy as she'd hoped, and it wasn't getting easier, either. Today, he'd decided to take a longer ride, and watching by the fence hadn't been an option. Brody was already mounted and waiting for her.

"Glad you decided to come," he said with a small smile.

"Not like I had a choice when you pointed west and said, 'Going that way. Send someone if I don't come back by sundown.'"

Brody chuckled and nudged Champ forward. "I've had enough of these canters around the field. I need to ride."

He'd had enough of careful perimeters, it seemed, and in a deep part of her, so had she. She was tired of being the responsible one, holding herself back, staying away. She wished she could just give in for a change and live to regret some poor decisions later. While it wasn't part of her nature to just let go like that, this ride was a welcome change of pace for them.

"How much pain are you in?" she asked.

Brody shot her a bland look. "Some."

"Scale of one to ten?" she prodded. He knew what she wanted to know, and his level of pain mattered. Pain in the body was a warning sign. Sometimes you had to push past it, but that was best done with physical therapy, not a hard ride into the country.

"I'm not telling you." Wry humor glinted in his eye. "You'll be happier that way. Trust me."

"You do realize that I can't pick you up or carry you back," she said drily.

Brody turned toward her, his dark eyes fastened on her face with a strangely tender look. "Kate, you don't have to carry me anywhere."

Brody kicked his horse into motion then recoiled. Kaitlyn wished she couldn't decipher all these hints about his discomfort. He was right—it would be easier not to know, especially since he wouldn't listen to her anyway. Brody was scanning the field ahead of them—tension in his shoulders. He was pushing himself past a different kind of pain threshold for this, too. He was riding like he had a gun trained on his back, his head constantly pivoting as he scanned the land ahead of them.

She heeled Mary Kay forward and caught up with Brody as they trotted out into the field. The horses snorted and Champ shook his head—they were eager to get moving. The sun was getting lower in the winter sky, but there was still plenty of daylight left. Kaitlyn drew in a breath that smelled of warm horse and freedom.

"You okay?" she asked.

"Fine." He glanced at her sideways, but then his gaze slid past her, behind her, around her...

"You're home," she reminded him. "No enemy here, Brody."

His dark gaze snapped back to her face and he let out a slow breath. "I know. Hard habit to break."

They could canter along here, Brody searching for invisible dangers, or they could ride. This wasn't the nurse in her making the call—this was the friend.

"You feel up to a gallop?" she asked.

A smile turned up one side of his mouth and they kicked their horses into motion. There was something about a galloping horse that made Kaitlyn's heart hover in her chest, joy crashing through her. She knew why Brody wanted to ride—really ride—but despite the enjoyment of a good gallop, she couldn't quite set to rest her nagging worry about his leg.

They slowed after a few minutes, and Kaitlyn found herself ahead of Brody this time. She turned in her saddle and looked back at him. He was tall and muscular, and in that saddle he looked as peaceful as she'd seen him since his return. His army time had stripped him of boyish playfulness and hardened him in ways she couldn't quite touch. If Nina had been able to get a snapshot of the man Brody would toughen into after his time in Afghanistan, would she have been so eager to move on with Brian? Brody had always been a handsome guy, but his honed strength made those good looks just a little less resistible.

"What?" he asked, noticing her scrutiny.

"Nothing."

"Liar."

She winced at that word. He was joking, but it stabbed a little deeper given their most recent history.

"Did you know that the army would change you this much?" she asked after a moment.

"Yeah." He eased his horse closer to hers, and he adjusted himself in the saddle with a suppressed wince. "They warn you about that, too. You'll never be the same. Once a soldier, always a soldier. It's kind of like being a cowboy—once it's in you, there's no going back. But they didn't tell me how lonely it would be."

His expression turned suddenly sad, and those steely eyes softened.

"Are you lonely?" she asked quietly.

"Aren't we all?"

It wasn't a direct answer, but it hinted at what lay beneath. What he'd seen, what he'd done and all those experiences that set him apart had also walled him off. No one could truly understand what he'd been through unless they were there. When he scanned the land like that, no one else saw the ghosts that he did.

"What about your friends?" she asked. "Have you heard from them?"

"I've heard from a few army buddies."

"What about your friends here?" she asked.

"I got a couple of phone calls. Mostly, people are uncomfortable."

That made sense. His friends had been Nina's friends, too. Breakups could be awkward, and even more so when you were a personal part of hiding it from a wounded vet.

"That's our fault, I think," Kaitlyn said. "We told them to keep a secret, but secrets only wedge people apart."

"Yeah, well, so do war stories."

Brody glanced at the sky, and Kaitlyn noticed that those scudding gray clouds had thickened and gathered, blocking out the wan sunlight. The wind picked up, too, whistling over the rolling plains ahead of them and whipping the snow into a tornado of glittering white. She shivered, hitching up her shoulders to protect her neck from the chilly probing fingers of the wind.

They rode in silence for quite some time, both in their own thoughts, and then the first snow started to fall.

"We should head back," Kaitlyn called, and Brody reined Champ in and looked over his shoulder the way they'd come, then up at the sky.

"The old barn is closer," he replied. "We can wait it out there."

Without waiting for her response, he pulled Champ around and headed north. Kaitlyn looked toward the ranch, now hidden behind the swell of a snow-washed hill, then sighed.

"Brody!" she called.

"Come on!" he shouted. "Or head back, if you want."

She remembered the old homestead from when they were kids. It was a rotting, sagging house next to a barn in similar condition. She hadn't seen it in a decade or more, and she was idly curious how much of it would still be standing. It was the house that Brody's great-great-grandfather had started out in… or had it been a great-great-uncle? She couldn't remember exactly.

Obviously, she wasn't going to leave him on his own, so she heeled Mary Kay into a trot and started closing the distance between her and Brody. He would have been better off with Aunt Bernice as his nurse— a middle-aged woman with some muscle and a flat stare. As it was, Kaitlyn didn't seem to have any ability to make Brody do what was good for him. And apparently, she didn't always want to.

He didn't look back once, but when she caught up he shot her a rueful smile.

"Last time we were out here, I kissed you."

He'd been all of twelve, and Kaitlyn had been ten at the time. The kiss had been chaste. Brody had pulled back and gone red, mumbled something about thinking she was pretty, and then picked up a rock and tossed it through a window. That same summer, Nina got her first bra, and the rest was history.

"We also broke windows," she reminded him with a soft laugh.

"I seem to remember that."

The snow was coming down more heavily now, and the wind whisked it back into their faces.

"Let's go!" Brody shouted over the wind, one hand holding his hat on his head, and they urged their horses into a gallop as they thundered across the field toward shelter.

THE SAGGING OLD barn rose like a blurry lump through the snowfall. Brody knew this land like the back of his hand, but it was different now. The hazy blur used to be comforting, but now it seemed ominous. Rubble, ruins and obscured vision were a lethal combination out there in the desert.

This isn't Afghanistan, he reminded himself. *I'm home. This is safe.*

It just didn't feel safe anymore. The cold wind angled through his jeans and chilled his hands through his gloves. He could hear Kaitlyn's horse close on his heels and when he glanced back, she was bent low, her hat down to shield her face from the blowing snow.

She'd asked for space and stuck to her boundaries. She came twice a day—once for riding and once for checking on his meds. She still claimed this lightening of her duties was for him. But he was too much— his pain was leaking over the edges and other people couldn't handle it. Even his nurse. Everyone wanted to be around the strong, capable cowboy, but the broken soldier was different. His very presence spoke of things no one wanted to think about too much.

The old house was farther off, the chimney standing tall despite the condition of the rest of the place.

He'd been thinking of this spot for a few days now...
wondering how much of it would still be standing.
The decrepit house used to capture his imagination
when he was young. Once he'd gone through the
house with his sister, and they'd found a few things
that must have belonged to their great-grandparents—
some spoons, a pair of rubber boots, a tin kettle, a
broken toaster. Nothing too romantic or intriguing,
but as a kid, it had brought that sagging house to life
again in his imagination—a link to the Masons' past.

He wouldn't go back into the house now. It
wouldn't be the same—he wouldn't be able to help
himself from scanning for booby traps and trip
wires...listening for that tiny click that came before
a detonation. Sometimes it was better to not torture
himself.

The middle of the barn roof was sunken in like an
old horse's back, a blanket of snow covering it almost
tenderly. The side sheds had since moldered and collapsed. The alley doors stood open, rusted hinges frozen in that position for decades. Champ shied back as
Brody urged him forward, but a swirl of frigid snow
changed the horse's mind and he obediently plodded
into the dim interior.

Brody stopped, let his eyes adjust and slowed his
breathing.

"What?" Kaitlyn followed close behind and dis-
mounted. "What's wrong?"

Nothing. Nothing was wrong. It was only the old
barn. He just had to remind himself of that. There'd

be a few rats, some mice, maybe even a bat or two, but no snipers, no dirty bombs.

His leg and hip were on fire. He guided Champ closer to a rail.

"Is that going to hold me?" he asked.

Kaitlyn gave it a shake. "Seems sturdy enough."

Dismounting was painful, but once he was on the ground, it felt good to move a bit. That was a good sign. He couldn't just stand here with that darkness at his back, though, and he limped to the open door and looked out at the drifting snowflakes. Wind howled through the eaves, but they were sheltered inside at least.

"How is your leg?"

Kaitlyn's voice pulled him back, and he shot her a wan smile. "About what you'd expect."

He knew she hated those vague answers, but his reticence wasn't about trying to hide his condition from her so much as trying to mentally suppress it himself. If he let the pain in and tried to accurately gauge how much it hurt, he'd lose that careful control he managed to maintain. Besides, his leg wasn't his biggest injury—he suffered more from what happened inside his own head.

Kaitlyn tugged an old bench into the splash of daylight, giving it one final heave until it was in position. Then she straightened.

"Sit," she said.

He didn't have it in him to argue, and he lowered himself onto the bench, his bad leg out straight in front of him. What he wouldn't give for that roaring fire right now. Kaitlyn sat next to him. She brushed the snow off her pants, then took off her hat and shook the snow from the rim before replacing it. Her face was pale in the dim light, and her jaw trembled slightly as she shivered.

"Come here," he said, and she scooted closer but still left a little gap between them. That wasn't going to do much good if they were going to keep each other warm. "All the way."

Kaitlyn scooted the last two inches so that her leg pressed against his and she fit perfectly under his arm, the warmth of her body mingling with his, rooting him to the present. This helped—keeping his brain in the here and now.

"This is highly unprofessional," she said after a moment.

"Probably." He chuckled, low and soft. "We'll go back to our careful distance when we're warm and dry. Deal?"

She felt good close against him, and it wasn't just a woman's touch, either. Granted, he'd been a year without it, but just any woman wouldn't have tugged down his defenses the way she did. There was something about her—the way she knew him too well, the way she didn't seem to act any part when she was with him.

Except nurse. But he grudgingly liked that challenge.

"The birthday party for our dads is at our place this year," Kaitlyn said.

"Yeah?" He wasn't sure what to say to that. It was

a tradition, and he'd been wanting to get back into the saddle for that trail ride. Somehow, things had changed since his return, and he wasn't as keen to do this.

"You'll come, won't you?" she asked.

Brody shook his head. "I know my dad would want me there, but I think I've let him down enough since I got back. Besides, sitting doing the birthday thing with Nina and Brian isn't high on my list of enjoyable activities."

Kaitlyn didn't answer, but he could tell she didn't like it. He couldn't see her face, so he pulled her hat off and tossed it beside them.

"What?" he said.

She pulled her fingers through her hair, tugging it away from her face. She was beautiful in that dim, stormy light. Her eyes were dark and luminous, and he found himself transfixed. The scent of her was so close, tugging at him despite his earnest effort to ignore it.

"You should come," she said.

"I really don't want to." He couldn't be much clearer than that. Breakups happened, but normally after your fiancée up and married someone else, a guy could count on family birthday parties without the in-person reminder.

"Okay, okay..." She sighed. "I do understand that. You know, Nina ruined things for all of us. She broke your heart—and I know that my complaints don't really compare—but I was looking forward to this birthday party." Her voice softened. "With you."

"I thought you wanted space," he said.

"I—" She stopped, color rising in her face. He'd caught her there.

"Didn't you?" he probed. "So why pull me into a family dinner?"

"It isn't just a family dinner. This is...tradition. We've done this party with our dads since we were all in diapers. I still miss...us." She shrugged weakly, and he wondered who was included in that word. Both families coming together, or something more intimate? "Brian isn't the same. He tries really hard, but... Anyway, they'll be back in Hope tomorrow, and we'll all have to face the new reality."

It did feel good to have Brian not measure up in some way. And did she say that Brian and Nina would be back in Hope as early as tomorrow? That little nugget of news hit him in a tender spot. He'd been getting over her, but seeing the happy couple wouldn't be easy.

"Glad to hear I rank higher for someone," he said with a note of bitterness in his tone.

"Well, you do." She fixed him with her direct, no-nonsense stare. "So I lost out on you as my brother-in-law, and I'm mad about that."

Brother-in-law. Yes, that was the plan, wasn't it? But right now, looking at her with her loose hair and eyes sparkling with emotion, he wasn't feeling all that brotherly. Had she always been like this—soft and open in a way that made him want to take some serious advantage?

"Brian does a fairly good Martha Stewart impression," he said, keeping his face deadpan. "There's always that."

Kaitlyn laughed and rolled her eyes. "Shut up, Brody."

That was the old Kaitlyn shining through—the Kaitlyn with the ponytail and the pile of books in front of her... He hadn't realized back then how much he'd counted on her to just be there. Teasing her, making her roll her eyes that way—it was a welcome relief.

"He also plays the spoons," Brody added. "I'm not even joking. And he sings in church. Like, very earnestly. You could always ask him to sing a hymn if things get slow."

Kaitlyn smacked his arm and shook her head. "Laugh it up, Brody, but I'm stuck with this guy in my family!"

And in a way, Brian had stolen that family from Brody, and he resented that. A lot. He'd been looking forward to family gatherings with Kaitlyn, too... mind you, now he was starting to see her in a whole new light.

"Nurses shouldn't smack their patients," he teased, but this time instead of laughing, she sobered. That hadn't been his intention, and he immediately regretted the words.

"No, they shouldn't," she agreed, and the open laughter seemed as far away as a dream. She cleared her throat and looked out toward the drifting snow.

"Kate..."

"You're right—"

"I was joking!" he exclaimed. "I've been trying to crack the whole nurse persona of yours since you arrived."

"It's not a persona, Brody. This is my profession."

He'd insulted her, and he hadn't meant to. He sighed and reached for her hand. She didn't reach back, but she also didn't pull away when his fingers closed around hers. He was tired of pretending that everything was okay, that his heart was intact, that his soul hadn't been scarred just as deeply as his leg in that explosion. He was tired of Kaitlyn being his nurse—always a few steps further than he wished she could be.

"Maybe I don't want to be your patient. Maybe I like it when you tell me to shut up and roll your eyes at me."

Maybe he liked it when she'd hold her breath because he was leaning over her, the way her lips parted when his breath tickled them. It was as simple as that, really. And add the fact that he was finding himself increasingly attracted to her…what was he supposed to do, just accept that everyone was going to treat him like a land mine, tiptoeing around him lest he go off? His body might be wounded, but he was still a man!

"You'll have to let me rebel a little bit, Kate," he said, his voice lowering. "I don't make a very meek patient."

"I'd noticed…" Her whisper was soft, and when she met his gaze this time, she'd lost that reserve, and he could see deeper emotions swimming under the surface. Those lips…why was it that when he looked at her pink rosebud mouth, the only thing that seemed logical was to kiss her?

When another gust of wind howled overhead, he suddenly realized that he didn't want to hold back anymore. He was single. So was she. She wanted to be on the clock as his nurse less often—perfect. He didn't feel like being nursed anyway. They were alone out here in this dilapidated barn, and the only thing he seemed capable of focusing on right now were those plump pink lips. He'd kissed her once when they were kids, and somehow he'd lost sight of her for far too long...but now he was seeing her again and he couldn't believe he'd let it go as long as he had.

He released her hand and slid his arm around her waist, pulling her closer to him so that she was pressed against his thigh. Her eyes widened in momentary surprise, and he dipped his head down, catching her lips with his. She moved into his kiss, her cool hand sliding around his neck. This felt more natural, more real, than her medical reserve. This was the kind of thing he'd been thinking about for days now—pulling her petite frame against him and feeling the rhythm of her heart through her body. Blood pounded in his ears, and while his leg ached something fierce, he wouldn't move for the world.

He slid his hand behind her neck, tugging her closer still, and the sensation of her hands moving down to his chest made him want to take this a whole lot further. But then she pushed him back, and as much as he wanted to simply follow her, close the distance again, he didn't. His lips felt moist where they'd been pressed against hers.

"No..." she said shakily.

Brody let her go, the word hitting him like a blow to the gut. "Why not?" he leaned toward her again, and she scooted back.

"Brody, I can't—"

"It's a kiss, Kate... I'm not asking for more than that."

She rose to her feet, anger sparking in her eyes. "Of course you aren't."

"Is this about me staying in Hope?" he asked uncertainly.

"No... Yes..." She heaved a sigh and shot him an annoyed look. "Given a choice, you'd be with my sister right now."

"What?" He blinked. Where did that come from? He hadn't been thinking about her sister at all.

"If she hadn't married Brian, you'd be planning your wedding right now, Brody. I know that—"

"But she did marry Brian." Were they going to fight about what might have happened if Nina hadn't dumped him? What was she expecting him to do, pine for the fiancée who was having a baby with his best friend?

"I'm your nurse," she said slowly, emotion choking her voice. "Your nurse, Brody."

And then it slammed home—she was here because she'd been hired to help with his recovery, and the wounds he was trying so desperately to ignore were right there in front of her. He wanted her to see the cowboy, the soldier, the man, but she saw the wounds, the patient. And that hurt more than Nina's thoughtless rejection. Nina hadn't wanted him at his best, and Kaitlyn had the chance to see the man in him and couldn't get past the wounds.

"Got it." He swallowed hard. "You're my nurse."

Silence stretched between them, and she adjusted her coat a little closer around her neck. Her cheeks were pink, and she didn't meet his eye. Fine. He'd made his point, and she'd made hers. He pushed himself to his feet and limped toward Champ.

"Where are you going?" she demanded.

"Home."

It might be snowing something fierce, but it was no worse than the elements he'd battled in Afghanistan. At least no one was shooting at him here. A little snow wouldn't kill a man, and he didn't think he could sit here and wait it out with Kaitlyn. Not like this.

At least he could save his parents some money and do without a nurse from now on. His wounds had closed, the stitches were out and he was pretty sure he could take it from here.

"I'm sorry about that kiss," he said, leading Champ to the rail that would help him to mount. "You're right. I overstepped. And obviously, I've recovered pretty well. You've done a good job on me. Maybe it's time for you to find a new post. I'll make sure my dad pays you out for the time he promised you."

Kaitlyn blinked, then shook her head. "Are you firing me?"

"It isn't you, Kate. You're a good nurse—more

than good, fantastic. But feeling like I do about you, do you really think having you working with me this closely is a good idea? When you put your hands on me, I feel things that would scandalize you, I'm sure. Just trust me on this. It's better."

He didn't wait for her answer. He knew he was right. They'd been teetering on the line between professional and personal long enough. He'd been pushing for her to see past the patient to the man, and he'd gotten his way. Mostly.

Unfortunately, she didn't want the man.

Chapter Eleven

The ride back to the ranch had been cold and dismal. The snow was already stopping, and the late-afternoon sunlight that peeked past the receding storm sparkled on fresh snow. Something had changed between them in that old barn, and Kaitlyn wasn't even sure she fully understood it. Brody was attracted to her, but she knew better than to give in to that. He was feeling attraction, but if she let herself go with him, she'd fall in love— the real, soul-deep kind of love. And he wouldn't.

Kaitlyn was Brody's second choice—she knew that. What kind of woman would she be to simply accept being Brody's temporary consolation prize?

But the kiss... That kiss had been just as tingling and heart-pounding as she'd imagined it a thousand times. This would be easier if their first real kiss— since she was a ten-year-old, at least—had been a disappointment, but it wasn't. That was cruelty in itself.

Before she'd left, Brody had reiterated what he'd said in the barn... *I'm a lot better than I was before. I don't need a nurse anymore. I can get physiotherapy at an office in Rickton. It's better this way, Kate.*

And a week ago, she might have breathed a sigh of relief, knowing she could step back and let her heart heal. Maybe it was already too late for that, because being dismissed had hurt on a deeper level than she'd imagined.

He didn't need her medical support anymore, and the kind of physical connection he was wanting, she couldn't give. She'd been in love with the wrong man for years. If she'd been smart, she would have found a nice guy somewhere and put her heart into forgetting Brody—ironically, like her sister had—but that was easier said than done.

THE NEXT DAY, Brian and Nina arrived. They drove up in a cherry red SUV and Kaitlyn opened the front door to welcome them. Nina was radiant in a cream-colored cowl-necked sweater that spilled over the front of a forest green wrap that hid her figure. Her makeup looked freshly touched up, a peach lipstick making her milky complexion look even softer against her voluminous red curls. She was even prettier now, if that were possible. It must be the pregnancy.

Brian carried himself a little more confidently than Kaitlyn remembered, his fresh face looking less boyish. They both seemed different now that they were married—more secure, perhaps. Nina and Brian exchanged a private smile as they came up to the door. Kaitlyn stepped back to let them in. Brian dropped their bags in the hallway and hugged Nina's mother, then shook her father's hand. Nina stood back, watching as her new husband greeted her family.

"How was the drive?" Ron Harpe asked.

"Good, good..." Brian nodded a couple of times. "The road was pretty clear, so no complaints."

"New vehicle?" Ron looked out the window, shading his eyes to get a better view.

"With the baby coming, we needed something more family friendly."

The men made small talk about weather and snow tires, and Kaitlyn, her mother and sister moved into the kitchen. It was the pattern they always followed—women in the kitchen, men elsewhere. It wasn't that the Harpe men couldn't cook—they could and did—it was just how they seemed to separate themselves.

"Look at you!" Tears welled in Sandra's eyes as she tugged Nina's wrap off. Nina's belly pushed against her soft sweater, her pregnancy more than obvious now. Kaitlyn stood back, watching her mother and sister hug. Nina had changed in the last couple of months. Not only did she look pregnant, but she looked gentler, too.

"Hi!" Nina said, coming up to hug Kaitlyn, and as she wrapped her arms around her sister, Kaitlyn felt tears of her own rising in her eyes.

So much had changed. Why couldn't they all just rewind a year and try this again? Kaitlyn released her sister and they exchanged a misty smile.

"So how are you feeling?" Kaitlyn asked.

"I'm constantly hungry," Nina replied. "And not just munchy. Like, if I don't eat, I get light-headed."

On cue, their mother pulled out a bowl of fresh muffins and nudged it in Nina's direction across the kitchen table. They sat down and Nina helped herself.

"How many weeks are you pregnant now?" their mother asked.

"Twenty-four." Nina blushed. "I'm over halfway there. Doesn't it seem like I should be bigger, or something?"

"It happens quickly enough," Sandra said. "Trust me. You'll be huge by the time this baby is born."

Looking at her sister, Kaitlyn couldn't imagine that huge state, but then Nina probably couldn't, either. Her sister and mom talked about pregnancy and all the feelings that went with it, and as Kaitlyn listened in silence, her mind kept going back to the cowboy her sister had left behind.

He'd fired her the day before, and Kaitlyn hadn't told anyone yet. Part of her was wondering if Brody would change his mind with a day on his own...and perhaps she was hoping he would. She was a glutton for punishment, apparently, because after that kiss, things would never just settle back to normal. She'd be smart to accept things as they were and move on.

"Mom said you've been taking care of Brody," Nina said, turning toward her. "How's he doing?"

Kaitlyn wasn't sure how to answer that. Brody was different, wounded. He wasn't the same guy who left, and Nina's betrayal mixed with his personal pain in a way she couldn't quite unwind. But how he was seemed almost too personal to chitchat about.

"He's recovering," she said simply.

"Is he mad?" Nina winced. "I don't blame him if he is."

"No," Kaitlyn said after a moment. "He isn't mad. He's…dealing with a lot right now, I guess."

"That's a relief." Nina reached for another muffin. "Because Brian is going to head over there and talk to him."

Kaitlyn blinked. Brian was going to waltz on over and surprise Brody with a little visit? If Brian was expecting to find a frail, wounded man, he'd have a surprise of his own. And she highly doubted that Brody was going to feel very welcoming of the buddy who'd betrayed him while he was off fighting.

"Are you sure that's a good idea?" Kaitlyn asked.

"They're men." Nina shrugged. "They'll sort it all out."

Nina had always had a deep faith in all things masculine. Men bent to her will and their testosterone worked in ways that made perfect sense to her. All the same, Nina looked nervously toward the window, as if she could see the Mason ranch five miles away.

"But Brody will be at the birthday party, right?" Nina said, turning back to Kaitlyn. "He'll see me pregnant, and he'll see Brian and he'll understand. It'll be a bit awkward, but I think it would help. Don't you?"

In that moment, looking at her sister's beautiful, hopeful, naive face, all of that anger she'd been sorting out and pushing down these last couple of weeks came bubbling up to the surface. Did Nina really believe that her beautiful, pregnant self was the balm for all of Brody's pain? Kaitlyn had wanted him to come so he wouldn't be alone, left out, isolated. But to gaze upon Nina? What made Nina think she still wielded that kind of power over him?

"Seriously?" Kaitlyn's voice shook as she tried to control her emotions. "Nina, do you know what you did to him? He came home with his leg torn to shreds and a prescription for painkillers, and he found out that his fiancée was married to his best friend. Then you hit him with the fact that you're pregnant!"

"*That* is not my fault," Nina retorted. "I'm not the one who wanted to hide it. I wanted to be up front about all of this from the beginning, but you all insisted that I keep my mouth shut!"

"So honest and virtuous." Kaitlyn couldn't help the drip of sarcasm. "You promised to marry him, and then cheated on him with his best friend."

"It wasn't like that." Tears choked off Nina's voice. "Brian and I—"

"I don't want to hear it." Kaitlyn scraped back her chair and stood. "Just don't think you're any expert on Brody Mason anymore. He's a different man now, and you crushed him. So carry on with your life, but don't think you can just smooth things over with a bat of your lashes."

"You little bi—" her sister started, but the word dried on her tongue as Kaitlyn met her gaze archly.

"Am I?" Kaitlyn asked blandly. "Because here's the sorry news for you, Nina. You're pregnant now. And married. You're officially boring and off the market. All those single men who fell over themselves to be near you? That's over. Because even if you don't, they've got some moral scruples."

Kaitlyn strode from the room, her sister's indignant voice following her as she headed for the door. She didn't know where she was going. Maybe she'd take a lesson from Brody and go for a ride.

She was angry—so angry she was shaking—and yet underneath that anger, she knew she was hurt. It wasn't only that her sister had broken Brody's heart, it was that she feared her sister was right, and that Nina would actually be able to mollify Brody with her charm and radiant beauty.

Brody had kissed Kaitlyn, and the memory of his lips on hers, his hands tugging her closer, closer, seared through her. She'd pulled back from that kiss for the same reason she was running from the house now…her sister held all the power when it came to Brody Mason's heart, and while that wasn't any surprise, and while she'd thought she'd prepared herself for it, it still stabbed.

Nina was married now, and pregnant. She had it all—a family of her own. And while Kaitlyn couldn't ever betray the depth of her feelings—although she hadn't exactly hidden it with her outburst in the kitchen—she longed to tell her sister to keep her hands off Brody Mason. He wasn't Nina's anymore.

Except Kaitlyn didn't have the right to do that. Brody wasn't hers, either—and he never had been.

BRODY LIMPED ACROSS the kitchen and grabbed a mug from the cabinet. It had been a long day without Kaitlyn. His parents had gone to town for a few errands, and his sister didn't live here anymore, as strange as that still felt. That left Brody on his own.

He'd gone out for a short ride, but it hadn't been as soothing as he'd hoped. His mind was spinning. With Kaitlyn here every day, life in Hope seemed like a possibility, even if he hadn't been ready to commit to it. Why she should be the glue for that plan, he had no idea. She was right that she was his nurse, and her presence on the Mason ranch had only been a temporary arrangement. He'd never asked her what her plans were for the future, and while she had more holding her here than he did, she was a free agent with her life ahead of her. And she knew she deserved better than him.

He hadn't told anyone that he'd fired Kaitlyn yet. They'd pay her out anyway, so he figured he'd leave that conversation for another day. Still, it hadn't been the same around here without Kaitlyn, and he missed her—even the way she effortlessly bossed him around.

"Get over it," he muttered to himself. He'd let himself get attached, and it ticked him off because he knew better. She'd been part of the deception, and she was Nina's sister. He knew every single reason why he should have kept his emotional distance, but he'd still kissed her.

And that made him an idiot.

There was a tap on the door and Brody turned, half expecting it to be Kaitlyn. He'd apologize—whatever good that would do. But when he opened the door, he stood face-to-face with Brian Dickerson. Brian was smaller, slimmer, with mouse-brown hair that spiked up in the back. He wore the same old leather jacket, but his jeans looked new. Crisp. Brody's mouth went dry, and he regarded the other man coldly until Brian shuffled his feet and looked down.

"Brian." He couldn't make his voice sound remotely welcoming. "What are you doing here?"

"Hey." Brian cleared his throat. "Can I come in?"

Brody considered saying no for a moment but then stepped back. Brian looked uncomfortable enough as it was, and Brody had a bone to pick with him. He was in a foul mood today, so Brian's timing was actually pretty good. If a man wanted to vent on someone, Brian was an ideal pick.

Brian looked almost frail next to Brody's broader army physique. Brody turned his back on him and went to finish preparing his coffee. He could hear the other man's boots shuffling on the kitchen floor.

"I guess we have some stuff to talk about," Brian said, and Brody turned, pinning the smaller man with an icy glare.

"Do we?"

"I came to say that I'm sorry," Brian said.

"Except you aren't," Brody retorted. "You're married. You're expecting a baby. You actually aren't sorry at all. You got the girl, right?"

Brian was silent, which was answer enough.

"Here's my problem," Brody said. "You were my best friend, and when I went to fight for our country, you moved in on my fiancée behind my back. I have a problem with that."

"I was in love with her," Brian said, and his voice sounded so plaintive that Brody believed him. Not that it made up for his betrayal. "I fully intended to keep my distance."

"So it's her fault?" Brody demanded. Not that he was actually placing blame. He wanted Brian to articulate exactly what he meant—no excuses.

"No." Brian's tone grew stronger. "It wasn't her fault. It wasn't mine. She fell in love with me, too. Things happened, Brody. I'm sorry."

Brody slammed down his mug and coffee sloshed over the side onto the countertop. "Do you know what it's like to come back from war to find out that the people you trusted most in the world had not only betrayed your trust, but lied to you for months?"

"It was to protect—"

"I know it was to protect me!" Brody shouted, and Brian's eyes widened and he took a step back. "I get that! But did you figure moving in on my fiancée would be the problem, not me finding out?"

He was angry, and he finally had the right person in front of him. Brian was the one who not only started up with Nina, but got her pregnant and married her. Then emailed for months, never once mentioning more than a movie he'd seen or idle gossip around town.

"She loves me, too," Brian said. "I didn't brainwash her. She finally spent some time with me alone. I had no intention of moving in on her. I was fully planning to do the honorable thing and step back and let her marry the better man, but…" Brian shook his head. "She felt the same way I did. I didn't see that coming."

Deep down, Brody knew Nina was probably happier with Brian, and that's the part that infuriated him the most. He even knew that he and Nina wouldn't have lasted after he'd gotten back. But it wasn't about Nina right now—Brian had betrayed their friendship.

"You never told me," Brody said. "You could have at any point."

"Tell my best friend I had a thing for his girl?" Brian belted out a bitter laugh. "No, I couldn't!"

"And when you realized you were in love?" Brody asked, crossing his arms over his chest. "Not even then?"

Brian looked away. "Again, you were already deployed, man. I couldn't do it."

And that was what everyone had told him—that once he was out there facing bullets, their hands had been tied. He'd been risking his life in the desert, and they'd all been solidifying their lies behind his back.

"If it could have happened any other way…" Brian spread his hands, then let them drop. "You don't believe me, and frankly, I wouldn't either in your position. But I'm sorry. Really sorry."

"You were my best friend," Brody said after a moment, and he swallowed hard against the emotion that threatened to choke him off.

"This doesn't have to erase our friendship," Brian

said. "Remember that time the Vernon cousins were going to beat you up?"

That wasn't fair—and it was a long time ago. They'd been all of twelve or thirteen and the Vernon cousins were hairy brutes who had Adam's apples by the age of nine. But Brian had refused to let Brody face them alone.

"You told your dad and he came and broke it up," Brody said. "Not your most heroic moment."

Truthfully, Brody had been grateful for the adult intervention, but he wasn't about to give Brian credit for anything right now.

"Yeah, well, you stayed in once piece, didn't you?" Brian asked with a small smile. "We were buddies, you and I. What about all those birthday parties and sleepovers? What about that time—"

"Enough!" Brody shook his head. "This isn't about times past, Brian. This is about the here and now. Do you know how many guys came by to see me when I got back?"

"I would have come by, but I didn't think you'd want me to—"

"None," Brody interrupted. "This leg—it changes things. Either the guys had moved on, or they made do with a phone call. But you get blown up, and people get uncomfortable."

Brian was silent, his gaze flickering down to Brody's leg. Let him look at it. He'd probably sport a limp for the rest of his life, and when he got old enough, it would be an old-timer story to tell—once there was distance enough that people stopped feeling awkward.

"I came back to silence, Brian. My fiancée was married. My best friend was gone. The other guys kept their distance." Brody's chin quivered and he fought back that rising emotion. "You were my best friend."

"I didn't know it was like that for you…" Brian's voice was thick. "I'm still here, Brody. I'm still your friend."

"No." Brody shook his head. "I had some real friends in the army. They got killed, but they were true-blue. You weren't."

Images of Jeff rose in his mind. Jeff, who would have taken a grenade to save any one of them… Jeff, whose shout of "I've got your back, man!" meant something.

Brody dashed the back of his hand across his eyes, wiping away a tear that had slipped past his defenses.

"Thanks for stopping by, but I'm done talking now. I'm pretty sure your wife will be wondering where you are."

"I'm sorry about the guys that didn't make it home," Brian said.

"Me, too." Brody sucked in a breath. "Now go back to Nina. Your duty's done."

Brian turned toward the door, his steps slowing to a stop as he put his hand on the knob. He turned back.

"Maybe you'll forgive me one day," Brian said.

"Don't count on it," Brody growled, and Brian met his gaze for a moment as if searching to see if Brody meant it. He didn't seem to find the encouragement he was looking for, because he turned then, hauled open the door and stepped out.

Brian didn't deserve to be let off the hook. He didn't deserve forgiveness or absolution for what he'd done. Let him squirm. He had it all—wife, baby on the way, a life free from haunting nightmares. Kaitlyn wasn't keen on Brian right now, but he knew her well enough to be sure that she'd warm up eventually. They'd find some common ground. Brian had it all...even Kaitlyn.

There was no way Brody could stay here in Hope. If he had any future at all, he needed to go back to the one place he knew he could trust someone's word— the army.

Chapter Twelve

Nina was wrong.

Her arrival could not heal Brody, and Nina had already proven that she wasn't good for him. So Kaitlyn's decision—to ask Brody to reconsider the party—wasn't about her sister at all, it was about Brody. Brody belonged in Hope, and he belonged with the people who loved him. Nina shouldn't be able to make their own hometown hero feel less than because she'd decided to show up. If anyone was going to be uncomfortable, let it be the cheating couple. Married or not, they were the ones with something to be ashamed of, not Brody.

So the next morning, while her mother was clattering around in the kitchen, starting on the big dinner, Kaitlyn hopped into her truck and made the short drive to the Mason ranch. This year, her father's birthday didn't seem festive, and that was hardly fair to him. He worked his fingers to the bone, and because of Nina and Brian, the atmosphere was strained, awkward.

"Do I call Millie?" her mother had asked, her

hands busy with a mixer and her voice raised to be heard over the motor. "She hasn't said anything is changed, but—maybe you could ask them about the party this year, Kaitlyn. You'll be there for your shift anyway, right? I need an approximate head count."

Her father had been in the mudroom, wiping his boots after a trip to the barn, pretending not to listen, but Kaitlyn knew better. He wouldn't let anyone see it, but he cared about these yearly parties. And when Kaitlyn poked her head around the doorway, his expression of false innocence was almost heartbreaking.

When Kaitlyn got to the Masons' side door, she could hear voices raised in volatile discussion before she even raised her hand to knock. She was about to slip away again—maybe come back at a better time—when the door flung open and she stared up into the stormy, reddened face of Ken Mason.

"You are not fired!" he bellowed, launched the screen door open and stepped back. "Get in here!"

Kaitlyn wasn't exactly keen on taking orders, and for a split second she was tempted to turn her back and walk away, but something stopped her—the sight of Brody behind his father, dark eyes pinned on her with unreadable emotion. So she did as she was commanded to do, kicked the snow off her boots and came inside. The entire Mason family stood in the kitchen. Mrs. Mason was by the coffeemaker, and Dakota was at the kitchen table looking mildly bored with the whole explosion. When Kaitlyn came inside, Brody crossed his arms over his chest, and she wondered if she'd made the wrong call. If Brody was having it out with his family, she really didn't belong in the middle of this.

"I'm sorry," Kaitlyn said, putting her hands up. "I know you don't want me here——"

"I hired you," Ken interrupted. "I pay you. Showing up was the right thing to do."

"And I'm the patient," Brody snapped. "I don't need babysitting."

Kaitlyn leaned against the closed door, unwilling to even unbutton her jacket. Her eyes were trained on Brody. He was angry—but this wasn't the kind of anger he'd shown toward the ranch hand who'd been hitting on her—this was something deeper and sadder.

"Take off your coat," Ken said, turning toward her. "And do whatever it is you do. You're on the clock, Kaitlyn."

"Hey," Kaitlyn said, raising her voice above the melee. "I didn't come here to force my services onto Brody."

"He needs medical care!" Ken retorted.

"Let her talk," Millie said, her voice quiet but carrying. "Why did you come, Kaitlyn?"

All eyes turned to her, and she felt her cheeks heat. "I…uh…"

What she'd come to say, she'd meant to say to Brody in private, and the Masons stared at her expectantly. She couldn't fix any of this, and she hadn't even been completely sure of what she'd say to Brody. She just knew she had to see him and sort things out somehow.

"I came to discuss the birthday dinner tonight," she said.

The room silenced, and then Dakota said, "Is that still on? I mean, all considering…"

"I told you already," Brody replied. "I'm not going."

"And if Brody isn't going, we aren't, either," Millie said.

Kaitlyn nodded. "I understand."

What else could she say? Of course, Brody's family would gather around him—as they should. And with Dakota's and Nina's new marriages, maybe it was time for all of this to change. Who was Kaitlyn to argue otherwise?

Ken stood in silence; his bluster seemed to have evaporated with the change of topic. He looked old and sad and he heaved a sigh.

"We've had this birthday weekend with the Harpes for what…thirty years now? And we can end all of that, but we can't change history. Nor can we change who our neighbors are. I think we should have this party as planned and if we change our minds for next year, then so be it. But if we cancel now, then it's over. And what do we have if we don't have neighbors we can count on?"

That was the country logic there—a community that pulled together regardless of spats or feuds. Ranchers needed their neighbors.

"Well…" Kaitlyn swallowed hard. "Maybe give us a call when you decide—"

"Wait." Brody ran a hand over his buzz-cut hair. "I want to talk to Kaitlyn alone."

Kaitlyn looked at Brody in surprise, and he met her gaze with a raised eyebrow of his own. He hobbled toward the door to the sitting room, then glanced back. Kaitlyn looked at Mr. and Mrs. Mason, then Dakota.

"Go on, now," Millie said, and hooked a thumb in her son's direction. "We need to sort this out if dinner plans are changing."

Kaitlyn could feel their eyes on her back as she crossed the kitchen and followed Brody into the sitting room. A fire had been kindled in the fireplace and Brody limped up next to it, but he didn't sit.

"I'm intruding," Kaitlyn said. "I shouldn't have come. I could have done this with a phone call."

Except that she'd been afraid if she did call, he would vanish somehow, and that would be the last she'd see of him. It wasn't logical, but tell her heart that.

"You're fine." Brody sighed. "Things are awkward anyway. So what happened with Nina?"

"Oh…" Kaitlyn sighed. "She's pregnant and glowing. And she's convinced you should come to the party for some sort of closure with her."

Did her resentment show through? It hardly seemed fair that Nina, who floated through life like a goddess, should also glow during her pregnancy. If life were fair at all, Nina would get horrible morning sickness and look green until she delivered, but life didn't seem to be landing on the side of fair. The baby was wonderful news, as all babies were, but couldn't

Nina have lost some of her smolder in the course of becoming a mother?

Brody rubbed a hand down his bad thigh and grimaced. "Brian came by."

"She mentioned he wanted to." Kaitlyn eyed him cautiously. "What did he want?"

"Wish I knew. He was sorry—or so he said. I don't know what he wanted from me—some kind of blessing? I have no idea."

Kaitlyn didn't know, either. How could any of them untangle this? Silence stretched between them. There were no solutions, just the fact that everything had changed.

"Is this it, then?" Kaitlyn asked. "Is this the end of birthday weekends for our dads and trail rides?"

Brody reached out and took her hand in his. "It couldn't stay the same forever, Kate."

She nodded, a lump in her throat. And he was right—it couldn't. All of them had tried to freeze it, hide it, keep it static, but that wasn't realistic.

"I wasn't completely honest before," she said.

"You don't say." He shot her a teasing smile. "What now?"

She smiled wanly at his little joke. She deserved it.

"I didn't tell my family that I'm not your nurse anymore." She shrugged uncomfortably. "I don't know why. So they think I'm here professionally right now."

"Sorry. I guess I could have figured out a way to let you save face," he said.

Saving face...yes, that would have been nice. But

Brody wasn't the one who pushed her into the shadows. He wasn't the one eclipsing her at every turn.

"My sister is newly married, Brody. And to top it off, she's also pregnant. If I was invisible before, can you imagine what the party will be like this year? Even my dad will be in the shadows. It's about Nina and her baby. And Brian, too...sort of. But my family will care significantly less about him than they do about the bun in the oven."

Brody's lips quirked up into a half smile. "You weren't invisible, Kate."

"Not to you." She shrugged weakly. Although he'd never seen what she'd hoped he'd see, at least he'd been her friend. "Anyway. It looks like we'll have a smaller party this year."

Brody's gaze moved toward the crackling fire. The orange light played over his rugged features, making him look older still and slightly haggard. He didn't need her burdens on top of his, and she felt a wave of remorse for having said anything at all.

"I'll go now," she said, breaking the stillness.

"Wait." Brody took a step toward her and reached out to move a tendril of hair away from her forehead. "What time is dinner?"

"Six, I think."

"Okay, then."

"Okay, then...what?" She fixed him with a stare, trying to decipher him. "Are you saying you'll come?"

"Yeah." He shrugged. "Everyone else can focus on Nina and her bun, and you and I can make fun of Brian. Maybe we can even convince him to sing a hymn."

Kaitlyn smiled. "You're cruel. I love it."

"This one's for you, Kate. I'll get you through the most awkward birthday party ever. What are friends for?"

"Okay." Her vision misted and she blinked it back. "Thank you, Brody. I'll save you a turkey leg. I'll guard it with my life."

"You better."

She turned toward the door, then paused and looked back. She wasn't sure what she wanted, but she loved him for this—a selfless act for her alone.

"You're still fired," he said.

She laughed and shook her head and headed for the door. When Kaitlyn emerged into the kitchen, Mr. and Mrs. Mason were sitting at the table with mugs of coffee in front of them. A jelly salad still in the mold sat at the end of the table closest to the door.

"So?" Ken asked with raised eyebrows.

"Brody is willing to come to the party..." She winced, realizing that none of this came down to her say so. "But I'm sure you'll need to discuss it as a family—"

"Dear, would you take that jelly salad to your mother?" Millie interrupted with a small smile. "I'll bring the rest when we arrive tonight for dinner."

Kaitlyn blinked, then nodded and picked up the dish. "Of course." She paused—uncertain of how much she should tell the Masons, but considering what they'd all been through for the last year, she decided to err on the side of transparency.

"He's quite firm about not wanting any more nursing care," she said. "And that's okay. He's doing fine on his own now. In my professional opinion, you don't need to worry too much."

"Oh, I know," Millie replied with exaggerated innocence. "We heard the whole conversation through the wall. It's like cardboard."

Kaitlyn blushed—so much for privacy. In a place the size of Hope with families as tight as these, privacy wasn't common. But the birthday party was going to happen, it seemed. The Masons and the Harpes would have one more celebration for the patriarchs of their families. It would likely be their last, so Kaitlyn would savor it.

This would be the time to say goodbye to her wistful hopes and take her future by the horns. Loving Brody wasn't going to just go away, but maybe while he got some closure with Nina, she could get some of her own.

Blast it. She hated it when Nina was right.

THAT EVENING, as they'd done for the last thirty years, the Mason and Harpe families came together for a birthday feast. The women had cooked all day. There was turkey, ham, stuffing, tiny roasted potatoes…the kind of food Brody had dreamed about while eating little plastic-wrapped army rations with his buddies and those massive camel spiders that could stop a man's heart if he came upon them without warning.

They drove the five miles to the Harpe Ranch carrying casserole dishes wrapped in bath towels to keep the contents hot. Brody held a bag of rolls and a couple bottles of wine, and he stood on the porch next to his family. The door swung open, and the festivities enveloped them.

There were hugs and pats on his arms as the older people greeted him. A couple of smaller boys stood by the wall, staring at him wide-eyed. He'd be the one their parents had been talking about, he realized wryly. Brody spotted Kaitlyn across the room. She wore a loose sand-colored sweater that accentuated the auburn waves tumbling over her shoulders. She stood with one hand in her back pocket, and her dark gaze was fixed on him with a strained expression.

Standing next to Kaitlyn was Nina—and he truly hadn't known how he'd feel looking at her again. She was as lovely as ever, except there was something intangibly different about how she held herself. She wasn't quite the same old Nina with that pinup-girl allure. Her belly was round and one porcelain hand lay on top of it. The moment Brody walked into the room he could see Brian tense up. He passed the dinner rolls and wine bottles to one of the aunts, made what he hoped were appropriate responses to the questions he couldn't quite make out, and moved in Kaitlyn's direction. A deal was a deal. Besides, she'd make this bearable for him, too.

The house was busy—there were a few other family members, some teenagers, a couple small kids having mashed potatoes early off plastic plates…the perfect homey scene that made him want to walk right back out of that house and go find some silence.

The soldier in him scanned the room for tensions and movements. Cowboys counted everything they passed—it was instinct based on years of ranching work. Soldiers, however, did more than count—they scanned for weapons, noticed bags, looked for shifting glances or a nervous jitter. An enemy could be anywhere.

Anywhere but in the Masons' living room, he reminded himself. This was awkward, but no one was going to try and kill him. Cowboy instincts would serve him better here, but his nerves were still jangly. There was the obvious handshaking, the hugs, the manly expressions of thanks for his service, the womanly questions about his comfort. And once he was past the aunts and uncles and had ruffled a few heads of smaller kids, he found himself facing the one woman he'd rather have avoided.

"Nina."

"Hi, Brody." The breathy, sexy voice was gone, and her gaze flickered toward Brian, then back again. "How are you?"

"Healing up," he said. "And you?"

Her hand moved over her stomach. "Really good."

Yeah, she would be. "Congratulations. You look... happy."

"Kaitlyn said you got my letter—"

"I got it." He glanced toward Kaitlyn and she was looking at her feet. "What's done is done, Nina. Brian's a good guy. You could have done worse."

"Oh, Brody," Nina sighed, putting a creamy hand on his arm. "You aren't worse. Just different, and I—"

And there she was—the real Nina. It never could have lasted between them. Nina could only have kept up her Marilyn Monroe act for so long before he'd been faced with the real woman over the breakfast table, or out in the fields or over a fence. And that would have been the real tragedy, when he realized he'd married a woman he didn't love half enough to be married to.

"I didn't mean me," he said incredulously, and Kaitlyn smothered a snort of laughter that she apparently tried to mask with a couple of fake coughs.

"Oh." Nina's cheeks turned pink and she shot her sister a glare. "Shut up, Kaitlyn."

And they were right back to being teenagers again, it seemed. No one had been able to unsettle Nina quite like Kaitlyn's utter refusal to accept her sister's status as sexpot. Kaitlyn composed herself and gave her sister a look so earnest that it was almost sincere, except Brody knew her well enough to recognize the roguish look in her eyes. Apparently, so did Nina, because she didn't look mollified.

"Nina, it's fine," Brody said. "A lot's changed. It was definitely a shock, but I'm all right. I wish you only the best."

"Well…thank you." Nina looked toward Brian again, and Brody nudged Kaitlyn's slippered foot with the toe of his boot. He was glad Kaitlyn was here to laugh at the ridiculousness of this whole situation. It helped, but he wanted out of this room.

"Brody, I was going to show you that thing," Kaitlyn said, and he shot her a grateful look.

"The thing?" he asked with exaggerated innocence. "Yes, of course."

There was no graceful way out of this, so it might as well be a blatantly obvious escape. He gave Nina an apologetic smile, then followed Kaitlyn. They emerged into the dining room, which was empty—thankfully—and he pulled out a chair and sank into it. Kaitlyn sat next to him, and they stared in silence at the table. A couple of vases were filled with carnations and baby's breath, and Mrs. Harpe's fine china glistened in the lowering light.

"Is this the thing?" Brody asked with a grim smile.

"Sorry, that was all I had. I'm not as good at the dramatic scenes as my sister is."

"Thank God." He leaned toward Kaitlyn and nudged her with his arm. In response, she tipped her head onto his strong shoulder, and it took all the self-control he had not to pull her into his arms. Instead, he leaned his cheek against her silky hair, and they sat there like that for a long moment. She made him feel stronger, saner.

The soft scent of her shampoo, the slight weight of her pressing into his arm and shoulder, comforted him more deeply than he cared to admit. His gaze moved around the familiar dining room and fell on a silver framed picture on the sideboard, and he knew what it was the moment he saw it.

"Is that their wedding?" he asked.

"What?" Kaitlyn took a moment, then straightened. "Oh! We were going to put that away."

All the comfort shattered in that moment. More hiding. More escaping. No, it was time to face things. He rose to his feet, his leg aching with the sudden movement, and he limped over to the picture and picked it up.

Nina made a beautiful bride, and her dress was more chaste than he'd imagined it would be. That must have been Brian's influence. Brian looked proud, scared, bashful—his cheeks were ruddy and he looked blissful, the idiot. It was a photo of the small wedding party—and Kaitlyn stood next to her sister. It wasn't surprising, but somehow he hadn't yet wondered about Kaitlyn's role in her sister's wedding.

"You were the maid of honor, weren't you?" he asked woodenly.

Kaitlyn was silent, and when he looked over at her, her expression said it all.

"I'm sorry," she said at last. "She's my sister. What was I supposed to do?"

And while he knew she was right, the silliness of this whole debacle evaporated and he was left staring at Kaitlyn as his heart sank within him. It wasn't the wedding itself that scraped back that protective barrier between his heart and reality, it was Kaitlyn. She'd stood by her sister, smiled in photos and silently given her approval to the biggest lie any of them had ever told.

"Did you email me that day?" he asked.

"What?" She shook her head. "No, I… That night,

I think. I just felt awful and I had to talk to you, so I sent an email."

"Yeah, I thought so."

Her emails were the ones that reassured him the most, and he would have breathed a sigh of relief at hearing from her on the very day it all went down. He'd trusted her more deeply than he'd even realized.

"Brody…"

"No." His throat was tight, and he pulled away as she reached for his arm.

"What would you have had me do?" she demanded, tears sparkling in her eyes. "She's my sister. Is she an idiot? Of course! But I knew that long before you did. And when family gets married, you make nice and you smile for the camera."

"And then you email the schmuck who's waiting for her."

Kaitlyn shook her head slowly, and he could see that she was biting back words, but he wanted to hear them. He'd had enough of this pussyfooting around the truth.

"Just say it!" he said.

"I told you before that you were dumb for even proposing." Her chin trembled and she balled her hands into fists.

"You never said dumb."

"Well, I'm saying it now." Anger snapped in her dark eyes. "Yes, I emailed you. I needed to hear back from you—to know you were okay. Do you have any idea what it feels like to wonder if someone is dead or alive? Well, I do! That entire bloody wedding I was thinking of you, and when it was done and I could finally escape to be by myself, I emailed you because I couldn't get you out of my head and I just wanted to hear something back."

Brody scrubbed a hand through his hair. What was she trying to say? Her eyes shone with something deeper, and as he looked down into her face with tears sparkling at the rims of her eyes and her lips quivering with the attempt to hold back her emotions, he knew what he wanted. It was all he could seem to think about whenever he was with her—whether it was good for him or not. He slid his hand behind her neck and pulled her closer, then dipped his head down and caught those quivering lips with his.

The kiss was bittersweet, filled with heartbreak and longing, and when she pulled back, he murmured, "I picked the wrong girl."

"I know." She wiped a tear from her cheek with the back of her hand. "I love you, Brody...for two years I loved you more than you'll ever know."

Her words struck him and he stared at her in shock. She'd been in love with him all that time? And he'd been treating her like a little sister, never once suspecting that she felt anything more for him than friendship. But he could see now that in her sweet, honest way she'd been more woman than her sister had ever been.

"If I'd known—"

"No!" Kaitlyn's voice turned fierce. "Don't even say it!"

Her eyes flashed fire and she shot him a look of warning.

"Why not?" he demanded. There had been enough hiding over the last year, enough cautious words. It was time to just say things like they were, because if there was one thing he'd learned from Afghanistan, it was that life was fleeting and words should never be wasted.

"Because it isn't true!" She took another step back. "You loved my sister, whether she was good for you or not, and if she'd waited for you, you'd be marrying her and I'd still be the little sister off to the side. So don't you say something you don't mean—"

"Do you love me still?" he interrupted her.

She didn't answer him, but her eyes were full of agony. He could see it written all over her—the blatantly obvious truth he'd missed when it mattered most. Kaitlyn was in love with him, and the realization was both humbling and terrifying.

"Because I've fallen for you, Kate—"

Not that it mattered right now. It didn't fix anything to realize it.

"You're attracted to me. That's different," she said with a shake of her head.

"I love you. It isn't different at all."

"What?" It was her turn to stare at him in shock.

"But I think we both know I'm not worth that risk." His heart ached almost physically as the words came out. "I'm a broken man in more ways than one. I'm not the same guy who left here."

"Yes, you are," she whispered. "You're the same

guy on the inside that you ever were. You're just more honest now."

He stepped closer to her, and while she didn't retreat, she shook her head.

"The worst part is, it doesn't matter," she said, swallowing hard. "If you'd had the choice, free and clear, you'd have married Nina. We both know it. It would have been the biggest mistake of your life, but you'd have done it and I would have lived my life in my sister's shadow. It doesn't matter. I can't be with you. I'm not going to be any man's second choice."

"So love me or not, you wouldn't have me," he said simply.

She didn't answer, and his heart sank. It was just as well. He should follow her example and bury these feelings.

"I'm going back to the army," he said after a moment.

"So you've decided, then?" she asked woodenly.

"I don't belong here, Kate," he said quietly. "You know that as well as I do. And what are we going to do...avoid each other? Pretend we don't feel this? Torment ourselves for the next few years? Am I supposed to watch you marry some other guy, too?"

His voice choked off. No, going back to the army was the right decision. He might not be fit for the front lines, but there would be a place for him somewhere, and his life would have meaning. Besides, he couldn't leave a family behind if something happened to him. That had been Jeff's biggest worry—what would happen to his wife and kids if he didn't come home… And that was a burden that Brody wouldn't put on to a woman. Kaitlyn had worried about him enough, and he wouldn't claim her heart only to make her live with that kind of uncertainty.

"And I couldn't ask you to be an army wife anyway. You're right to reject me first, Kate. I thought I wanted a woman waiting for me at home, but that was selfish. I'll never ask that of a woman again."

"Brody…" She didn't seem to know what to say, but a tear slipped down her cheek, and he reached up and brushed it away with the back of one finger.

"Make some excuse for me," he said. "I can't sit at this table and choke down turkey…"

He didn't wait for her answer—he didn't dare. He'd laid it all on the line for his country, and now he was walking way from the woman he'd fallen in love with. Sacrifice. Service. Why did it have to hurt so deeply? She wouldn't have her sister's seconds, and he wouldn't put her through a life of worry as an army wife. They were at an impasse.

So he walked out of the room, feeling her dewy eyes locked on to his back, and he forced himself to keep moving. If he paused, even for a moment, he'd walk right back over there and pull her into his arms no matter who was watching. One foot in front of the other—he knew how to force himself through pain. One step at a time.

He slipped out the side door and into the cold night. He'd go home. He'd try and get his head on straight. Kate deserved some happiness, and he was long past being able to provide it.

Chapter Thirteen

The next morning, Brody stood in the barn saddling up Champ. He hadn't intended to go for the trail ride. He could soldier through physical pain, but he wasn't as solid when it came to his heart. But Dakota and Andy had confronted him in the kitchen after breakfast. She said that with his plans for returning to the army and everything else that had changed, this would very likely be the last big birthday bash they did for Ken and Ron together. It was the end of an age, in a way. Besides, with Nina being pregnant she wouldn't be riding.

Dakota, like everyone else, had assumed it was Nina who'd done a number on him. But Nina wasn't the one making his chest ache this morning.

Falling in love with Kaitlyn hadn't been part of the plan, and it left him uncertain, muddled. Regardless of his feelings for Kaitlyn or Kaitlyn's for him, it couldn't work. There was no conquering this kind of miserable luck.

When he'd first arrived back home, his goal had been to do the trail ride with his dad. Besides, Brody was about to let his father down in the biggest way possible when he went back to the army—the least he could do was this one gesture.

He'd failed his last mission in Afghanistan, and he wasn't about to abandon this one because it was hard. He and Jeff used to joke about civilian problems— and this counted as one. He was doing this for his fallen buddies—the guys who wouldn't have any more chances with their own fathers. He owed them all.

Which brought him out to the barn on this frigid morning to saddle up his horse for the ride to the Harpe ranch with his family.

"Like old times," his mother said, pushing a hat onto her fluffy curls. "We probably won't have too many more like this, will we?"

His heart squeezed at the memories of years past— the Mason family riding together.

"Sure we will," his father retorted gruffly. "He's running the ranch with me."

His father's gravelly declaration didn't hold the same obstinate tenor it used to. Instead, Brody could hear a note of pleading in the older man's voice.

"Right?" His father shuffled his boots against the rocky ground, then fixed Brody with a stare. "Right, son?"

In that moment, Brody longed to say yes, that everything would be as close to normal as possible…that he'd butt heads with his dad for years to come, and he'd run the ranch just like his old man had done. That would comfort his parents and even make Dakota happy, but he couldn't do it. His mind was made up.

"I can't, Dad," he said, and in that moment, he was a kid again, longing for his father's approval. He just couldn't do what it would take to appease him. His father met his gaze for an agonizingly long minute and the older man's eyes misted. He blinked, cleared his throat and rubbed a hand over the stubble on his face, whiskers scratching audibly against calluses.

"Give it some thought, Brody. I can let you take over. For you, I could."

Brody knew exactly how hard it was for his father to even entertain stepping down, and he knew it was because his father wanted him home. He'd never supported Brody's dreams of army life, and after his injuries, his father would only worry more, because under all that gruff obstinacy was a heart that beat for his kids. But old dogs didn't learn new tricks, and Brody didn't think he deserved a life on the land anyway. He had mistakes to atone for and memories to bury. And that wouldn't come easy.

His father mounted, and the Mason family heeled their horses forward. An aching heart was a civilian problem. There were men who had given more than he ever had, and if they could have stuck around long enough to face some heartbreak, they'd have been grateful. Somehow, somewhere, he'd atone for his failure, and the next time he promised cover, he'd deliver or he'd die trying.

THE DAY MATCHED Kaitlyn's mood. Clouds hung low and tiny shards of snow drifted down from the sky like a mist of frozen tears. The wind was sharp and cold, biting into her knuckles, and she was grateful for the warmth of the horse beneath her. They'd been riding now for nearly an hour, and while being outside in nature was soothing, it hadn't eased the heaviness inside her. She'd thought that she'd grown used to that particular pain of loving a man she couldn't have, but apparently not. The burden had shifted, and it was rubbing her raw all over again.

Trees rose on either side, but she could see through the tangle of bare limbs, down a plummeting hill to the creek at the bottom. It burbled over rocks, and a few flat stones that rose above the water were covered in a layer of fresh snow. This was the same trail they rode every year, meandering up the foothills to a clearing that gave them a view of the rolling land. This was tradition. The celebration wasn't complete without that view.

This year, her heart was sodden in her chest, and even the prospect of that magnificent vista did nothing for her.

He said he loved me, too...

That made it harder, because how much love was enough? How much did he have to love her to overshadow what he'd shared with her sister? The night before, she'd lain in bed and gone over their words, that kiss, tried to remember every detail so she could piece it together, but she'd always come up with the same thing...he'd loved Nina first, and if Nina hadn't left him, Kaitlyn would be his sister-in-law and a good friend.

And if I didn't care? That was another question

that plagued her. What if she set her reservations aside? Could she love him enough to make up for the past? But even as she entertained the thought, she knew what her deepest fear was…that she'd be the runner-up, the second prize, the one Brody settled for when he couldn't have his heart's desire. And no matter how much she loved him, she couldn't make up for *that*.

Brody had come for the trail ride with his family, but besides the heavy sadness in his eyes, he'd barely spoken to her. It seemed that their words were used up last night. She could see the tensions playing around him, though. Mr. Mason looked older and sadder, and Mrs. Mason looked like she was trying to cheer them all up, but she wasn't fooling anyone. Dakota had Andy with her, and they talked in low tones as couples did.

Not everyone shared in the tension, though. Other family members and friends came on the annual trail ride, and the kids were chattering and laughing— weather couldn't dampen youthful enthusiasm. The older people seemed more inclined to silence or a comment or two as they plodded through the brush, but there was a general sense of satisfaction amongst the rest of the company, echoing the blessing said before last night's feast: make us truly thankful.

Kaitlyn glanced over her shoulder. Brian rode alone. Nina was at the house with their mother and Aunt Bernice making chili and biscuits for everyone for when they got back.

The snow was falling more heavily now, settling

on the rims of hats and then blowing away in a gust of icy wind. Kaitlyn pulled the rim of her hat down to shield her eyes, and she glanced around for the kids.

"Mark! Stay closer to the group!" she shouted to a boy who had ridden farther off.

"I'm in sight!" he called back. Mark was all of twelve, and he wanted his independence.

"It's snowing harder. One good gust, and you won't see a thing. Get closer!"

The boy complied and Kaitlyn urged her horse faster as she overtook some of the older people. They were all smart enough to keep to the trail—the kids were the problem.

"Becky! Olivia!"

Two of the girls had ridden down the slope to the creek. It wasn't deep, but if the snow thickened, it would be slippery to get back up the hill. These were kids who'd been riding since they were toddlers, but they were still kids and thought like kids.

"We're coming!" Olivia called.

Kaitlyn rode on. Another gust of frigid wind wound its way around her neck and she shivered. They'd probably be smart to turn back now.

"You okay?" Brody asked as she caught up to him, and for a moment, those dark eyes meeting hers brought a flood of relief. But she wouldn't let herself go—not again.

"I think it might be wise to head back," she said.

Before he could respond, her father called from ahead, "Let's turn back!" and Kaitlyn eased her horse into the trees to let the older people pass first. Brody followed her lead.

"I'll take up the rear," Kaitlyn said as a swirl of snow turned her world white for a moment, then cleared.

"I'll stay with you," Brody said.

"You need to get back to the house," she countered. "With this cold and your injuries—"

"You aren't my nurse anymore, Kate."

She couldn't make out his expression because he ducked his head against the elements, and she heaved a sigh. He was right, but she still felt responsible for the safety of this group.

"There are some girls down the ravine by the creek," Kaitlyn said. "I want to make sure they're back up to the trail. And Mark took off west... Did you see him?"

"There." Brody pointed and she could make out the kid's yellow jacket in the group farther ahead. He was with adults—that was what mattered. Brian reined his horse in where Kaitlyn and Brody stood as the last of the riders passed them. Brian wasn't an experienced rider. He'd been raised in the town of Hope, not on a ranch, and that made a difference in times like these. She felt a little sorry for him, though. He'd been riding alone—attempting to keep up with his new in-laws. He probably had a few hopeful expectations about this trail ride, too, and Kaitlyn was pretty sure it wasn't exactly living up to them.

"Brian, we're heading back," Kaitlyn said. "Just stick to the trail. The snow makes things trickier."

Brian tugged on his horse's reins, but the horse didn't budge. He tugged a little harder, and irritation welled up inside of her. Couldn't Nina have chosen a guy who could at least handle a horse? Brian was nice enough, but she didn't have time to babysit her new brother-in-law, either.

"I've got to make sure the girls are out of the ravine," Kaitlyn said, straining her eyes down the slope, but she couldn't see that far and the snow swirled dangerously. The wind picked up, whisking her words away as she said them. There wasn't time for this.

"Go," Brody said. "I'll take up the rear with Brian."

"You sure?" He had done a lot of healing but the cold wouldn't be good for his leg. She had a sudden swell of misgiving.

"Go!" Brody's voice held an order. "There's no time. Get the girls and we'll meet up with you in the pasture."

Kaitlyn met his gaze and saw steely reserve there. She was worrying about him because she was in the habit of doing so, and this wasn't the time for sorting through her emotions. Brody wasn't hers to worry about, and he'd made that clear enough the night before. There were kids that needed to be accounted for, and Brody was right—there was no time.

"Okay…" She gathered up her reins. "I'll see you there."

And she kicked her horse into motion.

"Olivia!" she shouted. "Becky!"

There was no answer, and she pushed forward into the ever-thickening snow. She took one last look back and saw Brody's gaze fixed on her, his expression granite, but his eyes betrayed the turmoil under that stubborn reserve.

He felt it, too.

Chapter Fourteen

A swirl of snow obliterated Kaitlyn from view, and for a split second, Brody felt like he was back on the front lines again. Except Afghanistan was hot, and the wind there whipped up sand instead of snow, but that feeling of isolation was the same—exposed to the elements, blinded by the wind, his shoulder blades tingling, waiting for the bullet of some unseen enemy. There was always the chance that a sniper was patiently waiting, crosshairs on your back...

He could remember several times when he'd made a dash for it as bullets whistled past his head. Three more inches, and he would have been dead. And then there was the time Jeff shot a sniper that had him in the crosshairs while he was relieving himself. He'd survived Afghanistan, but sometimes he wondered how he'd managed it. There was the backup provided by a good buddy, but it wasn't just that... Of all the men who didn't make it, why had he?

"Brody—" Brian was looking at him, concern on his face. "You okay, man?"

"Fine." Brody shot him what he hoped passed for

an annoyed look. These moments came upon him unexpectedly, swallowing his emotions in a different time and place. He sucked in a wavering breath and rotated his shoulders, refocusing on the man in front of him. Brian was watching him closely—too closely, and now the annoyance was genuine. He wasn't a danger to anyone out here. He wasn't going to suddenly snap, or something.

"You sure? You look…kind of pale."

Great. The last thing he needed was for Brian to see weakness. Brian's horse's ears flattened against its head as a low howl of wind circled around them. Brian should be worrying a little more about his horse and a little less about him.

"Let's get your horse out of the trees. He doesn't like being hemmed in."

Brody leaned forward to grab the bridle, and his leg burned in protest. He still felt vulnerable, his back exposed. Anxiety simmered just under the surface, and he tried to push it back, but that never worked. It wasn't a matter of sheer mental force. It took self-reminders.

There were no snipers in these woods. There was no enemy. He was on American soil—safe. His brain knew this, but his body hadn't adjusted to the new normal yet.

"How's your leg?" Brian asked.

So he assumed it was physical pain? Just as well Brian didn't guess at how deep all this went.

"Better than it was," Brody said wryly.

"I heard it was bad," Brian said. "You said you lost some buddies in that explosion, too."

"You want to talk about that here?" Brody demanded. That was personal, and Brian had lost all rights to ask anything personal.

"You should talk to someone," Brian said.

"Not you." They exchanged a long look, then Brody nodded toward the horse. "Let me take the reins and I'll lead you out to the path—"

The wind moaned, the sound coming from every direction at once. The horse's eyes rolled in terror, and it pawed at the ground, whinnying and rearing up. A branch overhead creaked, and Brody's leg spasmed. His cold fingers fumbled with the leather and he clenched his teeth against the pain, but as he let go of the bridle, Brian's horse spun and bolted into the trees.

It all happened so quickly that Brody was left staring at Brian's back as the horse galloped away.

Brody muttered an oath and his heartbeat sped up, but this time it was warranted. Brian was on a spooked horse running pell-mell into a forest in the middle of blinding snow. He had a choice—go back to the trail and hope that Brian's horse would find its way out of the forest, or go after them.

I've got your back, man...

Brody had made the promise as Jeff crept into the empty road, and Brody had sat there in the shelter of the truck's shade, his gun trained on the shrubs and shadows ahead. If one so much as moved, he'd send a bullet straight into it, but it hadn't been a sniper that time…it had been a mine.

A soldier didn't leave another soldier out there alone—no one left behind. In battle, you did what you had to do.

Digging his heels into Champ's sides, Brody wheeled the stallion around and plunged into the woods in the direction Brian had disappeared.

KAITLYN SHOOK THE snow from her jacket and kicked her boots against the step. The horses were being groomed by the stable hands, and the kids were already in the living room chattering about their adventure. Mark was telling the story of not being able to see a thing and having to follow the sound of voices to get back to the trail, but the wind kept whipping their calls in every direction.

Yes, quite the adventure. Kaitlyn hung her hat on a peg and shut the door behind her. Youthful enthusiasm didn't take into account that being caught in a blizzard when the temperature plunged could be fatal.

"Are Brody and Brian back?" Kaitlyn called into the kitchen.

"What?" Nina came to the doorway and looked around the mudroom. "Aren't they with you?"

A rock of worry settled into Kaitlyn's belly and she shook her head. "They were coming up behind while I went to make sure the girls got up from the creek—" She rubbed her cold hands together. "I was held up trying to get Becky's horse over a slippery spot where she couldn't get footing, so when I didn't see Brody and Brian at the pasture, I'd assumed they'd come on ahead of us."

"They aren't here." Nina's voice wavered. "Brian doesn't know those woods—"

"—but Brody does," Sandra Harpe countered, coming into the mudroom. "Brody is an army-trained soldier and he knows that land. If anyone is qualified to bring Brian back, it's Brody."

But Brody was wounded, and Kaitlyn could see that the same thing had occurred to both her mother and sister. Brody had taken up the rear with Brian, but there was a man recovering from a serious injury with a man who didn't know the woods...and they hadn't come back.

"I'm going to find them—" Nina grabbed a coat, and Kaitlyn and her mother exchanged a look. It was a nice sentiment, but a pregnant woman wasn't going to do much on her own besides harm her baby.

"You'd better stay," their mother said. "You're pregnant. Now is not the time to push it. The men will go look, but you'd better stay."

"I'm supposed to just sit here?" Nina demanded. "My husband is out there, and people die in blizzards, Mom. I'm going!"

For once, Kaitlyn agreed with her sister. She wasn't about to sit in the house and wait on someone else to find them, either.

"I'm going, too," Kaitlyn said with a shake of her head. "I'll take her in the truck with me. Don't worry, she'll be fine."

"Tell the others," Sandra said, her tone turning

brisk. "I'll keep the kids here, and the rest of you go together. You two aren't going alone, either. Ron!" She turned away, calling her husband. "Ron! Brody and Brian are still out there!"

The next few minutes were spent with hurried explanations and plans being made for the aunts and uncles to form a search party along the edge of the woods. They'd bring rope to tie around their waists so they could find their way back again, and flashlights—as much use as they'd be in that blinding snow.

Before ten minutes had passed, Kaitlyn and Nina were in the ranch truck, bumping down the gravel road toward the pasture. Kaitlyn knew this stretch better than anyone, and she could drive it blindfolded if necessary, but still she leaned forward, clutching the steering wheel and squinting to see as much as possible through the swirling snowflakes. Windshield wipers whipped back and forth in a futile effort to clear their view.

"I begged Brian not to go with you," Nina said bitterly. "He should have stayed with me. I told him it would be no use. All he wanted was a chance to bond with the family..."

Guilt pricked at Kaitlyn's composure. She'd noticed Brian's attempts to make nice, but she'd had bigger things on her mind. Nina was right—he'd been on that ride to fit in, make a start with the family, and while a few uncles had chatted with him a bit, he hadn't made much headway. And Kaitlyn hadn't done much to make him feel welcome. To be honest, he wasn't terribly welcome. He'd swooped in and taken something that wasn't his, and while Nina had married him, everyone else knew the truth. And if there were sides to take, Kaitlyn landed solidly on Brody's. As ironic as that was, considering that she was in love with the man...

"It's the timing," Kaitlyn said. "You two waltz back right when Brody is back from Afghanistan. I can't speak for anyone else, but I was focused on my own problems."

"Yours?" Nina snapped. "What problems?"

Was her sister serious? Did she really think that Kaitlyn had no problems of her own? Nina's problems were of her own making...she stirred up drama everywhere she stepped!

"Brody?" Nina guessed. "Is that it? Everyone's so worried about how Brody was going to take it? I get it, but what you don't know—"

"Do you really get it?" Kaitlyn shot back. "Because you didn't seem to be thinking about him at all!"

Kaitlyn had been, though. Not an hour passed during the last year that Kaitlyn hadn't been thinking about Brody and praying for his safety. Someone had to...his fiancée sure didn't seem inclined.

"I was doing what I had to do!" Nina's voice rose. "Do you really think I'm some slut who fell into bed with Brian out of boredom?"

Kaitlyn was stunned, and her gaze flickered in her sister's direction to catch Nina's angry glare.

"Kind of," Kaitlyn said. "You were engaged to the sweetest cowboy around, and you couldn't wait until he got back. So yeah, that pretty much covers what all of us thought."

And could Nina really blame them? Nina had everything—natural beauty, sultry allure, magnetism that drew people to her—and she couldn't wait a few months for the man she'd promised to marry. What kind of woman did that?

"Nice." Nina's tone dripped disdain. "Did you know that Brody didn't want to marry me?"

That seemed awfully convenient for Nina, but Kaitlyn knew better. "That isn't true. He came home expecting to marry you. I know that for a fact."

"Expecting to do something and wanting it are two different things," Nina said. "He said it over and over again—he'd promised and he'd follow through, but he made it sound more like a duty than a pleasure."

"He proposed because he loved you," Kaitlyn said. "I was there. I saw the whole thing. No one forced him into that."

"And after he got to Afghanistan, things changed." Nina heaved a sigh. "He changed. But you're right— he's a good guy, and he believes in doing the right thing. He'd married me, but it would have been biting the bullet to do it. Do you really think I wanted to be a man's duty and obligation?"

Was this true? Nina seemed to believe it.

"I saved some of the emails. I'll show them to you when we get back. But Brian was different," Nina said, and her voice thickened with emotion. "I wasn't a duty, I was... I was the best thing to ever happen to him. So forgive me if I fell in love."

"I *thought* you were in love with Brody." Hadn't her sister claimed to be in love over and over again when she showed off the ring? Love—the real thing—wasn't as fickle as that.

"I thought I was, until I experienced the real thing. I loved Brody, but I wasn't in love with him..."

And that was what had bothered her all along with her sister's treatment of Brody. She hadn't loved him—not like Kaitlyn had. She'd cared more about makeup, friends, shopping, appearances...anything seemed to rank higher than Brody did, and that had been wrong. She'd chalked it up to Nina's general shallowness, but had it been simpler still—had Nina simply not been in love?

"He would have married you, though," Kaitlyn said.

"And I'd have driven him crazy," Nina said quietly. "I wasn't enough. And a pretty face ages eventually, you know. I couldn't go through with it, even if he'd been willing to be miserable to keep his promise. I couldn't do it to him, and I bloody well couldn't do it to myself."

"But Brian makes you happy?"

"Brian makes me more than happy, he makes me... confident. He loves me, Kaitlyn—not the clothes or the makeup, or any of that. He loves me. I could be dressed in a paper bag and he'd get that goofy look on his face."

"That's the way it's supposed to be," Kaitlyn admitted. That was the very feeling she longed for with Brody—confidence in his love.

"If it had been Brian over there in Afghanistan," Nina said, her voice low. "I'd have waited. I'd have waited for a decade for him to come home to me."

If Brody had changed like Nina said—if he'd planned to go through with the wedding out of duty instead of devotion—that might change things for Kaitlyn. But the heartbreaking part was that even if she wanted to be with him, Brody was going back to the army, and he'd said that he wouldn't ask any woman to be a military wife.

Kaitlyn slowed as they approached the edge of the woods, then put her headlights on high beam. The wind picked up as they rumbled up to the tree line, shrieking through the bare limbs. Nina unbuckled her seat belt and pushed open the door before the truck was even stopped.

"Hold on!" Kaitlyn said. "Don't forget that you're pregnant, Nina."

"My husband is out there—" Nina's voice shook. "And every minute counts. So quit mollycoddling me, and let's get them home."

Kaitlyn understood her sister all too well. She had a man out there whom she loved, too. She could only pray that they'd be able to find them before the temperature dropped. If two women standing outside in the snow could make a difference, then they would. They'd stand out there shouting the names that filled their hearts, while the rest of the search team delved into the woods.

If only for once love could be enough.

And then she saw it—the brown coat of Brian's horse standing in the shelter of the trees...riderless and alone.

Chapter Fifteen

The air grew steadily colder as Brody rode. He couldn't hear the crash of Brian's horse ahead of him anymore, and the path he'd taken was less obvious now. He reined in his horse and listened.

"Brian!" he shouted, but the wind whipped the word away from his mouth. Movement in the corner of his eye drew his attention, and he paused, waiting for the swirling snow to abate for a moment. The wind whistled harder, and then there was a break just long enough for him to make out a voice in reply, but he couldn't catch the words. Brian was here... somewhere.

He kept a tight hold on the reins, listening and watching, and then he saw it again—a bush shaking. Brody pulled left and heeled Champ forward.

The wind rose once more and Brody ducked his head against the stinging pellets of snow. His hip and thigh were on fire, but his mind was clear and focused on the mission at hand. The Brian he was searching for wasn't the man who'd betrayed him...he was the buddy who'd come for sleepovers and ridden with him in the back of the rusted pickup truck, the friend he'd laughed with and talked with, the conspirator from his youth. Suddenly, out here in the driving snow and plummeting cold, things seemed clearer and simpler.

Choices—did he really have as many as he'd thought? His mind kept going back to the villagers—the ones he couldn't save because he'd been one man with one gun, and sometimes a spray of bullets only hurt more people. He wasn't God. He was one man. He couldn't see it all. He couldn't fix it all.

Champ balked and the blowing snow slowed again to reveal an arm... The sight of the hand just visible outside the brush brought bile up in his throat—mingled with heart-wrenching memories. He dreamed of that hand every night... But then the hand moved, and Brian raised his head.

A flood of relief shot new strength through Brody's tired limbs, and he swung from the saddle, landing with a grunt and an oath as the pain stabbed deep into his groin.

"Are you okay?" Brody asked, sinking to his knees next to the man.

"I'm pretty sure I broke my ankle." Brian winced as he tried to sit up, then sank back down. "I can't move."

"You'll have to," Brody retorted. "Let me see..."

He ran his hands down Brian's leg, and one foot was at an odd angle. That would be a bad break... If he were on a combat mission, he'd be stabbing a syringe of morphine into the man's thigh and giving him a wave of pain relief, but he didn't come prepared for the battlefield.

"It's bad, right?" Brian's voice was weakening.

"A scratch," Brody said. "You'll be fine. Quit your whining."

Brian smiled wanly. "I'm warming up, actually."

"No, you aren't," Brody said. That was the cold settling into him, and if he was starting to feel warm then they were on borrowed time. The shock wouldn't help matters, either. "Now, we're going to get you onto my horse."

"No—" Brian swallowed hard. "I can't make it."

"You bloody well can!" Brody retorted. "If your wife can give birth a few months from now, then you can take it like a man. Because if you stay out here, you're going to freeze to death before anyone finds us. And while we have some history, man, I don't feel like dying with you. Got it?"

Brody felt his pockets. He had a couple of pain pills left. They wouldn't be enough to dull this level of agony, but they'd help. He pulled them out and shook them into his palm.

"Chew these," Brody ordered. "They'll take the edge off faster that way."

Brian didn't argue, and crunched the pills that Brody pushed into his mouth. After a couple of minutes, the smaller man's eyes turned slightly glassy.

"Better?" Brody asked.

"I still feel it," Brian moaned. "But I care less."

"That'll do..." Brody grabbed Brian's arms and

wound them around his neck. "Now, on three we're getting up. I'm getting you home."

He didn't wait for an agreement—Brian wasn't going to get a vote on this one. He was bringing Brian back to his wife, and that was that. Brian could curse him for a cruel SOB for the rest of his life if he felt so inclined, and he very well might with the level of pain Brian was about to endure, but he was getting on that horse.

Brian let out a cry as Brody hauled him up, and then the smaller man mercifully passed out. That was the point Brody had been waiting for—unconsciousness. Brody heaved him across the saddle like a sack of grain. If there was mercy above, Brian would stay unconscious until they got back, because every jolt of that horse was going to bring fresh agony.

If he could have done this for Jeff, he would have. Jeff would have cursed him with creative eloquence, but his wife would have gotten her husband back alive, and those kids would have had their dad. If he could have done this for every single Afghani villager, he would have, too. But he was just one man… and that spray of bullets wasn't the salvation he'd hoped for.

One man simply could not save the world. Damn it. Tears welled in his eyes. For the first time, the knowledge settled into him—he wasn't ever going to be enough for a job that big. Some jobs required a whole army for a reason, whole platoons of men and women doing their jobs together, and even then, there would be a few cracks in the armor.

"I'm not enough," he said aloud, his voice choked with tears, but it was a relief to finally let them out. Maybe it was all right to be just one man. Maybe he could forgive himself for being less than an army.

Far away, carried by the wind and possibly conjured up in his mind, he heard Kaitlyn's voice calling his name, calling him home.

I've got your back, man. Whether Brian wanted it or not.

He'd never make up for lives lost, but maybe he could atone for some of that guilt. And for all the people he'd not been hero enough for, he hoped they could forgive him—wherever they had ended up. Kaitlyn had called him brave on that tattered Valentine card, and perhaps the truest bravery was living with all these memories locked in his head, the bloody reminders that he was just one guy. And maybe, if he could accept his own limitations, he could learn to forgive himself.

For the first time since Jeff's death, Brody felt the burden lift, and it was like that shadowy ghost of his friend finally slipped away to a better place.

Rest in peace, man. You did your best.

Maybe Brody could find some peace, too…

KAITLYN HEARD THE shout go up when the men found Brody and Brian. They came out of the forest, Brody limping badly ahead of the horse, and Brian flopped across the saddle. Kaitlyn burst into a run, sprinting toward them as Brody's bad leg gave out and he collapsed to the ground.

The uncles grabbed him under the arms and helped him back to his feet while other friendly hands eased Brian down from the saddle.

"Brian's ankle is broken. He's in shock, and his core temperature is down," Brody said. Kaitlyn's eyes whipped from Brody to Brian, and before she had to decide on which man to give her attention to first, Aunt Bernice—the more experienced nurse—dropped to her knees next to Brian and began inspecting him.

"Brody!" Kaitlyn gasped, and he opened his arms as she flung herself into them. He closed her in his iron grasp, pulling her hard against him.

"Kate... I could have sworn I heard you calling..."

Tears welled up in her eyes, and she pulled back, putting her attention down to his leg. He'd pushed too hard, and she could only imagine what damage he'd done to himself.

"How badly does it hurt?" she whispered.

"Shut up." He laughed hoarsely. "I'll let you nurse me to your heart's content later. But first—" And his lips came down onto hers, pinning her to the spot, claiming her as his. He pressed her closer against his broad chest, the steady beat of his heart lulling her into his embrace.

When he finally released her, Kaitlyn found herself a little weak-kneed. She glanced toward Brian, who had come to, moaning in pain as Nina and Aunt Bernice leaned over him.

"Is he going to be okay?" Kaitlyn asked.

"Yeah. His ankle is broken pretty badly, but he'll

be fine." Brody gave a wry smile. "I got him home. Mission accomplished."

Nina looked up from her crouched position next to her husband, and she smiled mistily toward them. She mouthed the words *Thank you* and then turned back to Brian, clutching his hand in hers. Brian was looking up at her, his face ashen with pain. They'd found the real deal, Nina and Brian, and Kaitlyn knew just how lucky that was. Kaitlyn had found a true love, too, but life wasn't always nurturing of a heart's desire.

"She loves him…" Brody said quietly.

"Yeah." Kaitlyn swallowed hard. "More than life."

"Kate…" Brody reached into his front pocket and pulled out that faded old Valentine. "You're the one who got me through. Do you know that?"

"And you're going back…" His words the day before were seared into her heart. He'd go back to the army, and she'd go back to trying to stop loving him. It was almost too painful to bear.

"I'm staying," he said. "My dad has been asking me to stick around and run the ranch with him. It means a lot to him… I hoped you might be okay with it, too."

She frowned, his words slowly sinking in. "What? So you won't go back to the army?"

"No. I made my peace with a few things out there in the woods. I'm going to have to forgive myself for not being enough…for anyone. I did my best—"

Enough…he worried about not being enough? Maybe he hadn't been enough for Nina, and maybe he couldn't pull off being a one-man army, but when it came to being everything a woman desired, he measured up and then some…he just hadn't seen it.

"You were always enough for me." Her voice choked with tears. No man had ever measured up to him, and no man ever would.

"Any way you'd reconsider and give us a chance?" he asked quietly. His voice was low, and his dark eyes were pinned to hers pleadingly. "I don't know what I'd have to do to convince you that you have me, heart and soul…"

She longed to say yes, but uncertainty swelled inside her. There was something she had to know.

"Nina had the distinct impression that you'd have been marrying her out of duty," Kaitlyn said slowly. "Is that true?"

He paused, then nodded. "Yeah, once I was over there… That's the thing—that war changed me. I wasn't the same guy who left—not in the ways that worked with Nina and me. The army stripped off the cocky veneer and left me raw. I might have done my duty, Kate, but I'd still have fallen for you. I wasn't going to be able to help that. Besides—" He nodded in the direction of Nina and Brian. "Those two belong together."

They did—Kaitlyn had to agree. Her sister had found the right man for her, and she'd blossomed because of it.

"Kate…" Brody ran the back of his finger down her cheek. "I love you. And if the only good thing to come out of being nearly blown up was to see that you were the one for me, then my pain was worth it. I'm staying, and if you'll have me, I'll spend the rest of my life proving that you're the only one I need. And if you won't have me, I'm still spending the rest of my life proving it."

Kaitlyn felt her eyes mist with tears. "You are a stubborn lout, Brody Mason."

"Guilty." He smiled tenderly down at her and cupped her face in his hand. "Knowing just how stubborn I am, how about you save us both the frustration and just marry me already?"

She blinked, her breath caught in her throat.

"If you could put up with some ex-army cowboy," he murmured. "I'll still be stubborn and I'll probably never lose this limp, but I'd be the luckiest guy on the planet, and I'd never forget it."

"Yes." She nodded, a smile bursting through her tears, and his lips came down onto hers once more. She wrapped her arms around his neck and let herself go in those strong arms. Loving him hadn't been a choice, and stopping her feelings wasn't even an option. But marrying him…that was her choice for better or for worse for the rest of her life.

Epilogue

Standing at the front of the church on Valentine's Day, Brody's heart was in his throat.

Kaitlyn had given him a new Valentine after they got engaged, and this one showed a little bride and groom roasting sausages over a fire. It said, "The wurst part is waiting for you." He'd laughed, and he had a sneaking suspicion they'd just started a tradition of cheesy Valentines that would last a lifetime. But nothing could take the place of the simple gesture of love that got him through the war: *You're brave, Valentine.*

Kaitlyn hadn't told him a thing about the dress, claiming that there weren't enough surprises in the world. They'd thrown this wedding together in less than two weeks, and he had no idea what to expect. The doors opened once more, and as the music swelled, he caught a glimpse of the most beautiful woman he'd ever seen. Kaitlyn's dark auburn waves hung down her shoulders, and her eyes were alight. She sucked in a wavering breath, then looked over at Ron Harpe.

Brody was marrying a whole family, too, and he had no doubt they'd be on his doorstep—just as quickly as he'd be on Andy's—if he ever did wrong by Kate. But that wouldn't happen. He'd promised to show her just how much he loved her, and it would take a lifetime to demonstrate.

Her dress was a pale ivory that clung to her narrow waist. It was a shorter dress, calf length, reminding him of the '40s styles he'd seen in family photos, and it made his overly serious Kate look even lovelier. A simple green ribbon was tied around her waist, matching the green-and-white bouquet in her hands. The very sight of her left him breathless, and he knew he was beyond lucky to be able to claim her as his. Mrs. Kaitlyn Mason...but she'd always be his own Kate. He couldn't wait to slide the diamond band onto her finger and say his *I do*s.

Brody might not be an army, but to one woman, he was the whole world. He'd make a vow to her—to support and love her for as long as they both should live. He'd promise to put her happiness before his own, and he'd honor that...every day of his life. And when he saw a smile light up her face, he'd know he was doing something right.

Don't call him a hero—just call him grateful.

* * * * *

MILLS & BOON®

Cherish™

EXPERIENCE THE ULTIMATE RUSH OF FALLING IN LOVE

A sneak peek at next month's titles...

In stores from 9th February 2017:

- **Proposal for the Wedding Planner** – Sophie Pembroke *and* **Fortune's Second-Chance Cowboy** – Marie Ferrarella
- **Return of Her Italian Duke** – Rebecca Winters *and* **The Marine Makes His Match** – Victoria Pade

In stores from 23rd February 2017:

- **The Millionaire's Royal Rescue** – Jennifer Faye *and* **Just a Little Bit Married** – Teresa Southwick
- **A Bride for the Brooding Boss** – Bella Bucannon *and* **Kiss Me, Sheriff!** – Wendy Warren

Just can't wait?
Buy our books online before they hit the shops!
www.millsandboon.co.uk

Also available as eBooks.

MILLS & BOON®

EXCLUSIVE EXTRACT

Pastry chef Gemma Rizzo never expected
to see Vincenzo Gagliardi again. And now
he's not just the duke who left her
broken-hearted… he's her boss!

Read on for a sneak preview of
RETURN OF HER ITALIAN DUKE

Since he'd returned to Italy, thoughts of Gemma had
come back full force. At times he'd been so preoccupied,
the guys were probably ready to give up on him. To
think that after all this time and searching for her, she
was right here. Bracing himself, he took the few steps
necessary to reach Takis's office.

With the door ajar he could see a polished-looking
woman in a blue-and-white suit with dark honey-blond
hair falling to her shoulders. She stood near the desk
with her head bowed, so he couldn't yet see her profile.

Vincenzo swallowed hard to realize Gemma was no
longer the teenager with short hair he used to spot when
she came bounding up the stone steps of the *castello*
from school wearing her uniform. She'd grown into a
curvaceous woman.

"Gemma." He said her name, but it came out gravelly.

A sharp intake of breath reverberated in the office.
She wheeled around. Those unforgettable brilliant green
eyes with the darker green rims fastened on him. A

stillness seemed to surround her. She grabbed hold of the desk.

"Vincenzo—I—I think I must be hallucinating."

"I'm in the same condition." His gaze fell on the lips he'd kissed that unforgettable night. Their shape hadn't changed, nor the lovely mold of her facial features.

She appeared to have trouble catching her breath. "What's going on? I don't understand."

"Please sit down and I'll tell you."

He could see she was trembling. When she didn't do his bidding, he said, "I have a better idea. Let's go for a ride in my car. It's parked out front. We'll drive to the lake at the back of the estate, where no one will bother us. Maybe by the time we reach it, your shock will have worn off enough to talk to me."

Hectic color spilled into her cheeks. "Surely you're joking. After ten years of silence, you suddenly show up here this morning, honestly thinking I would go anywhere with you?"

Don't miss
RETURN OF HER ITALIAN DUKE
by Rebecca Winters

Available March 2017
www.millsandboon.co.uk

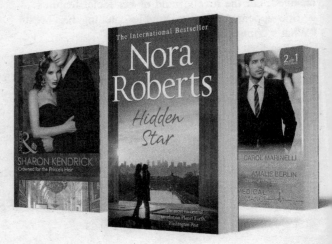

Join Britain's BIGGEST Romance Book Club

- **EXCLUSIVE offers every month**
- **FREE delivery direct to your door**
- **NEVER MISS a title**
- **EARN Bonus Book points**

Call Customer Services
0844 844 1358*

or visit
illsandboon.co.uk/subscriptions